RAINBOW magic ®

The Sporty Fairies

For Aphra O'Brien
with lots of love

Special thanks to
Sue Mongredien

ORCHARD BOOKS

First published in Great Britain in 2009 by
Orchard Books
This edition published in 2017 by
The Watts Publishing Group

1

A CIP catalogue record for this book is available from the British Library.

ISBN 978 1 40835 321 9

Printed in Great Britain by Clays Ltd, St Ives plc

The paper and board used in this book are made from wood from responsible sources

Orchard Books
An imprint of Hachette Children's Group
Part of The Watts Publishing Group Limited
Carmelite House, 50 Victoria Embankment, London EC4Y 0DZ

An Hachette UK Company
www.hachette.co.uk
www.hachettechildrens.co.uk

Helena
the Horseriding
Fairy

by Daisy Meadows

Join the **Rainbow Magic Reading Challenge!**

Read the story and collect your fairy points to climb the
Reading Rainbow at the back of the book.

This book is worth 5 points.

The Fairyland Palace

Fairyla

Car Park

Coaches

Cooke Football Stadium

Riding Stables

Netball Courts

Tippington Town

Football Pitches

LEISURE CENTRE

Swimming Pool

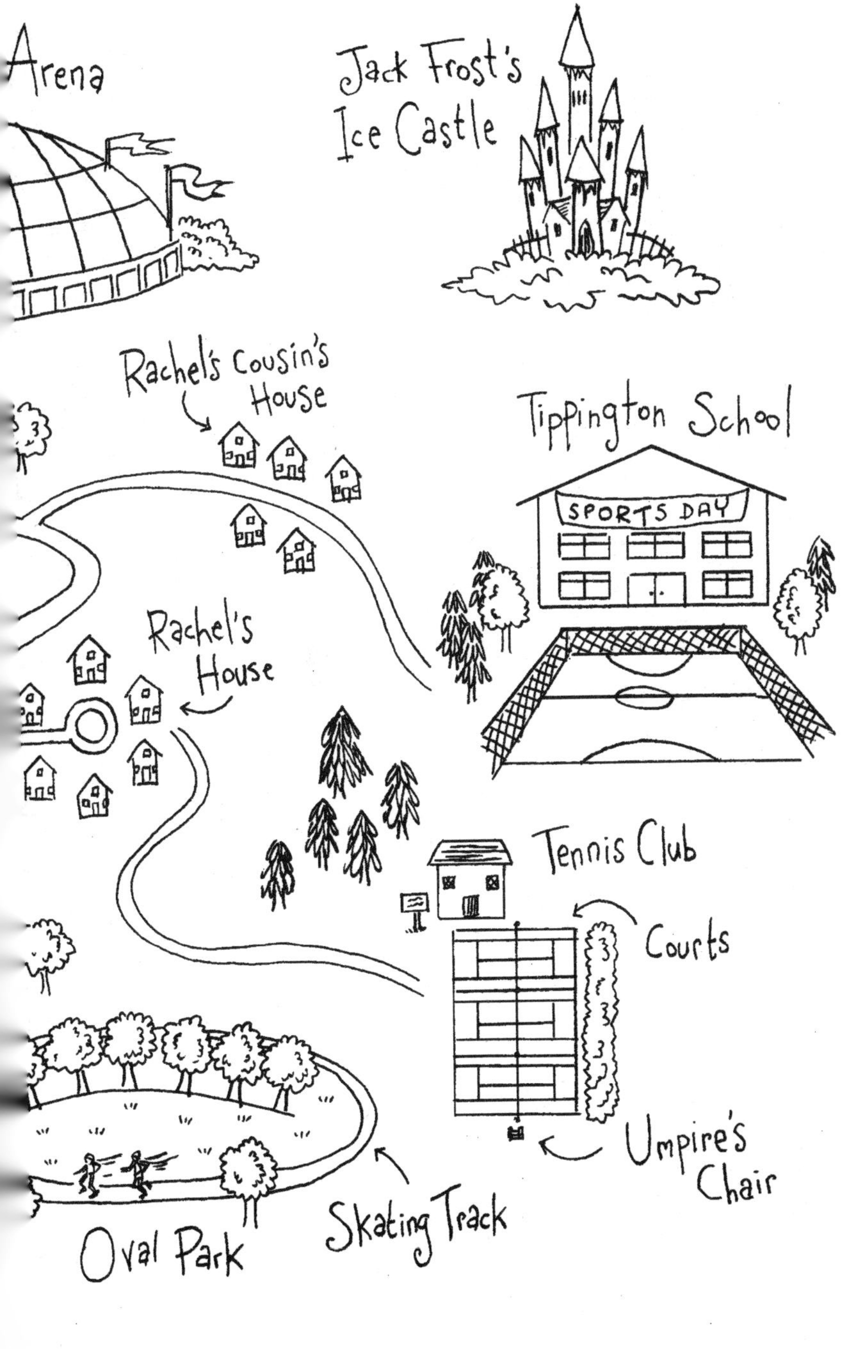

Arena

Jack Frost's
Ice Castle

Rachel's Cousin's
House

Tippington School

SPORTS DAY

Rachel's
House

Tennis Club

Courts

Umpire's
Chair

Oval Park

Skating Track

The Fairyland Olympics are about to start,
And my crafty goblins are going to take part.
We'll win this year, for I've got a cunning plan.
I'm sending my goblins to the arena in Fairyland.

The Magic Sporty Objects that make sports safe and fun,
Will be stolen by my goblins, to keep until we've won.
Sporty Fairies, prepare to lose and to watch us win.
Goblins, follow my commands, and let the games begin!

Contents

Magic Message

"There," Rachel Walker said, tidying her hair. "I'm ready. Are you?"

Kirsty Tate buttoned her jodhpurs and smiled at her best friend. "Yes," she said. "I can't wait!"

It was the first day of the Easter holidays, and Kirsty had come to stay with Rachel's family for a week.

In a few minutes, they would be setting off for a riding lesson at the Tippington Stables, and both girls were looking forward to it. They always seemed to have the best fun when they were together – and the most exciting adventures.

Kirsty was just about to open the door, when something caught her eye. The pages of Rachel's diary were fluttering as it lay on her bed, and yet there was no breeze in the room. "Rachel!" she said, pointing. "Look!"

She and Rachel ran over excitedly. They had each been given matching bejewelled diaries by the King and Queen of Fairyland, as thank-you presents for helping the fairies. The two girls had been friends with the fairies long enough now to know that the fluttering pages of the book meant only one thing: something magical was about to happen!

Kirsty held her breath as the diary fell open at two blank pages, and then she gasped as sparkly gold writing appeared on the paper, letter by letter.

"It's a message," Rachel whispered, her heart pounding.

We…need…your…help! the golden letters spelled.

We need your help...

"The fairies must be in trouble!"
Kirsty cried. "Do you think Jack Frost
has been up to more mischief?"

"There's only one way to find out,"
Rachel said, and Kirsty nodded.

Both girls opened the golden lockets
around their necks, and took out pinches
of fairy dust.

"Let's go to Fairyland," said Kirsty,
flinging the fairy dust over herself.

"To Fairyland!" Rachel echoed, doing the same, and the two girls were immediately swept up in a magical whirlwind of rainbow-coloured sparkles. As they were whisked along, they felt themselves shrinking to become fairies. Kirsty smiled as she glanced over her shoulder and saw a pair of delicate, gossamer wings on her back, glittering with magic.

Seconds later, they were set down
gently in Fairyland, in front of
an unfamiliar building.
It was very grand, with
white marble walls
and glittering golden
pillars at the front.

King Oberon
and Queen
Titania stepped
forward to greet
the girls, with seven
other fairies that
Rachel and Kirsty
didn't recognise.

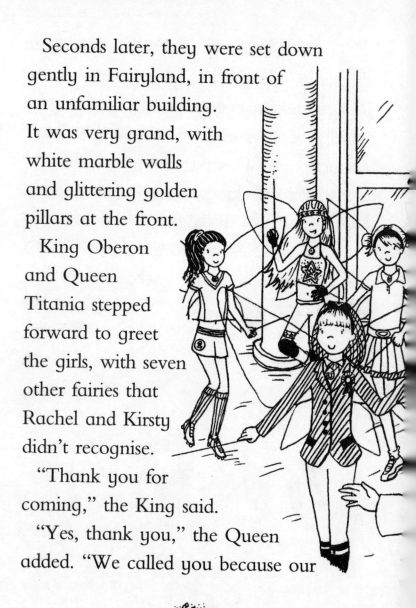

"Thank you for
coming," the King said.

"Yes, thank you," the Queen
added. "We called you because our

Sporty Fairies really need your help." She gestured to the fairies who stood nearby and introduced them. "This is Helena the Horseriding Fairy, Francesca the Football Fairy, Zoe the Skating Fairy, Naomi the Netball Fairy, Samantha the Swimming Fairy, Alice the Tennis Fairy and Gemma the Gymnastics Fairy." Each fairy smiled and said hello, looking pleased to see Rachel and Kirsty.

"Hello," Rachel said, curtseying to the King and Queen and smiling at the Sporty Fairies. Then she looked around curiously. "Um... Where are we? I don't recognise this part of Fairyland."

"This is the Fairyland Arena," Helena explained, "where all the sporting events take place."

"Come and see," the Queen said, waving at the golden doors. They swung open immediately, and Kirsty and Rachel followed the fairies through to a large stadium. There were rows of white seats surrounding a football pitch of the greenest grass the girls had ever seen.

"Wow," Kirsty breathed. "My dad would love this!"

"That's not all," Samantha told them. "If we need to change it for a different sport, we just do this…" She waved her wand and a stream of sparkly fairy dust billowed out. The football pitch gleamed a bright gold, and a rainbow-coloured mist descended upon it. Then the mist cleared, and, where the grass had been seconds before, there was now a swimming pool, its turquoise water shimmering in the sunshine.

Rachel blinked. "That's amazing!" she marvelled.

The Queen smiled. "Our Sporty Fairies help make sports fun and exciting, both in Fairyland and in the human world," she explained.

"And we also make sure sporting events run smoothly, and that everyone plays fairly," added Zoe.

"How do you manage that?"
Kirsty asked.

"With our Magic Sporty Objects,"
Francesca told her. "I have a Magic
Football, Gemma has a Magic Hoop,
Alice has a Magic Tennis Racquet…"

"Not any more, though," Alice chipped
in sadly. "Because our Magic Sporty
Objects have been stolen!"

Burglars Break In

"Stolen?" echoed Kirsty. "What happened?"

"Well," Naomi began, "when we're not using our magic objects, we keep them in our lockers here at the arena. But when we came to collect them this morning, the lockers were empty!"

"So who could have taken them?" Rachel asked. Then she sighed.

She already knew the answer.

Gemma nodded, as if reading Rachel's mind. "Yes," she said. "Jack Frost and his goblins. We have special keys that open our lockers," – she showed the girls a tiny key, shaped like a bow, that she wore on a silver chain around her neck – "and we think Jack Frost used his special ice magic to forge copies of them."

"Then he sent his goblins to break into our lockers and steal our magic objects," Zoe went on.

22

"Let's go to the seeing pool," Queen Titania suggested. "Then we can watch how it happened." She waved her wand and they were all whisked up in a sparkly magic whirlwind which took them to the edge of a clear blue pool in the palace gardens. The queen waved her wand once more, and the pool rippled with colour.

The girls watched as images appeared on the water. There were the seven Sporty Fairies flying towards the arena at dawn, the sun streaking the sky orange and red. Down below were

several goblins: one stumbling as he
kicked a football, two others trying
to throw a netball to each other, but
missing every time, and others falling
over as they practised handstands and
cartwheels. Kirsty and Rachel watched
as the Sporty Fairies flew down towards
the goblins.

"We always try to help anyone if they're struggling at sport," Francesca explained.

"But it was all a trick," Gemma sighed. "The goblins were just trying to distract us, and keep us away from the locker room!"

The water in the pool rippled and the
image changed again. Now Rachel and
Kirsty could see seven goblins, dressed in
black with balaclavas on their heads,
climbing a rope up a wall towards an
open window in the arena. They kept
slipping and treading on each other but,
eventually, they all scrambled in
through the window.

"That's the window of the locker room," Samantha told the girls. "*Our* locker room!"

Once inside, the tallest goblin shouted, "Ice keys at the ready!" and each goblin took an icy key from his pocket and tried it in the locker before him.

There was chaos at first, as the goblins couldn't find the right doors for their keys, but eventually they got there. As the last key went in, all seven doors sprang open, revealing the Magic Sporty Objects inside: a hard hat, a football, a skate lace, a netball, goggles, a tennis racquet and a hoop – all sparkling with fairy magic.

Each goblin grabbed one of the Magic Sporty Objects eagerly.

"Now, remember what Jack Frost told us," the tallest goblin said. "If we're going to win the Fairyland Olympics, we need to practise our sports with the other goblins. But make sure you keep the magic objects well hidden in the human world while you practise so the fairies can't find them! Then, in a week, we'll come back to Fairyland...and win the Olympics!"

The other goblins cheered and then
they all sprinted back to the window.
Rachel couldn't help noticing how much
more athletic they
seemed now that they
had the Magic
Sporty Objects.
The goblin with
the hoop even
did a series of
backflips across the floor!

Then the scene in the pool faded,
and the water became clear again.

"The Fairyland Olympics start in seven
days," King Oberon explained, "and
Jack Frost knows that when the Magic
Sporty Objects are away from the Sporty
Fairies, or their lockers, sporting events
will be ruined everywhere, because

nobody will be able to enjoy sports
as usual."

The Queen nodded. "He also knows that
the Magic Sporty Objects are so powerful
that they make anyone near them perform
very well at sport," she added. "He wants
his goblins to win the Olympics, so he can
get his hands on the prize."

"What is the prize?" Kirsty asked.

"The Fairyland Olympics Cup,"
the Queen replied. "It's filled with
luck – which would mean Jack Frost could
get away with all sorts of new mischief!"

"Can the Olympics be
cancelled until the Magic
Sporty Objects are found?"
Rachel suggested.

"No," the King sighed.
"The Fairyland Olympics

are linked to the human Olympics. If we cancel our event, it would cause great disruption to the ones in your world."

"That's right," Zoe said. "But while we don't have our magical objects, nobody will be able to play well."

"Nobody will be enjoying sport very much either," Francesca added.

"We've just got to get our objects back," Naomi cried. "Otherwise both Olympic Games, and all sports, will be ruined!"

Girls on the Case

"We'll help you in any way we can," Rachel said at once.

"Thank you," Helena replied. "We know the goblins will be practising their new skills, so it's likely they'll turn up in places connected with each object."

"We're going riding today," Kirsty remembered. "Maybe the goblin with

your Magic Hard Hat will be there,
Helena." In her green riding jacket,
cream jodhpurs and boots, Kirsty
thought Helena was dressed perfectly
for riding, except that she was missing

the special hard hat
that all riders need.
Helena looked
excited. "I'll
come with you
in case he is,"
she said. "Let's
go back to your
world straight away!"

The girls just had time to say
goodbye to the fairies before Helena
waved her wand and whisked them
back to Rachel's room, turning the girls
back to their normal sizes once more.

"Are you ready, girls?" they heard
Mr Walker calling.

Helena tucked herself into Kirsty's
pocket and the girls hurried downstairs.
Rachel's dad was waiting to drive them
to the stables. Both girls felt tingly with
excitement as they got into the car; it
was wonderful to be starting a new
fairy adventure!

It was only a short ride to Tippington Stables and soon Mr Walker was parking the car.

"Have fun," he told the girls as they jumped out. "I'll come and pick you up at the end of your lesson."

"Bye, Dad!" Rachel called. She turned to Kirsty. "Our instructor is called Vivian," she said. "Let's go and find her."

As the girls walked towards the stables, Helena peeked out of Kirsty's pocket. "I can sense a lot of disruption here," she said anxiously. "I wonder what's going on."

Rachel and Kirsty walked in through the stable yard entrance and then stopped in horror at the chaos that greeted them. Horses and ponies were trotting to and fro without riders while the stable hands ran around trying to catch them. One girl was trying to mount, but the girth on her pony hadn't been done up tightly enough so the saddle immediately slipped, tipping the rider straight off onto the ground.

Kirsty helped the girl to her feet.
Luckily she was unhurt and thanked
Kirsty before going back to her horse.

A lady with red hair bustled over,
and Helena ducked down into Kirsty's
pocket again.

"Hello, Vivian," Rachel said to
the red-haired lady. "Is everything...
all right?"

Vivian sighed. "I'm afraid it's rather hectic today, girls!" she said, "but I'm trying to sort everything out before your lesson. You're on Shadow, Rachel, and your friend, Kirsty, will be on Brandy. Why don't you go and tack up? I'll be with you as soon as I've got everything under control."

"OK," Rachel said, as she and Kirsty set off to find their ponies. They'd hardly taken a step when a rider went careering past – sitting the wrong way round on her pony.

"Oh, no!" Vivian cried, rushing to help. "I'll meet you in the paddock, girls!" she called over her shoulder.

Helena peeked out again. "This is awful," she said despairingly. "And it's all because my Magic Hard Hat is missing. If I had that, then none of this would be happening!" Suddenly she frowned as if she was deep in concentration. Then her tiny face brightened. "It's here," she said in her clear silvery voice. "My Magic Hard Hat is here – I can sense it." She stared in dismay as another horse trotted past without a rider on its back. "But we've got to find it soon," she added, "before things get any worse!"

A Sweet Idea

Rachel and Kirsty went to tack up, keeping an eye out for any goblins that might have Helena's Magic Hard Hat.

"Good boy, Brandy," Kirsty said, patting her toffee-coloured pony as she adjusted her stirrups. Brandy tossed his head impatiently as Kirsty attempted to get the stirrups even, but one of

the stirrup leathers just wouldn't go
any shorter.

"Ah!" said Helena, flying on to
Kirsty's shoulder. "It's because my hat
is missing that you're having so much
trouble, but I know a trick that might
help. If you twist the strap around the
stirrup, it'll make it a little shorter.
Watch!" She waved her wand and
Kirsty watched in delight
as the stirrup leather
came undone,
looped itself
through the
stirrup and then
did itself up
again, making
the stirrups
perfectly even.

"Thank you, Helena," Kirsty smiled.

Meanwhile, Rachel was having trouble getting Shadow to take the bit in his mouth.

"Everything's more difficult because my hat's missing," Helena sighed. "Let me try, Rachel." She hovered close to Shadow's left ear and spoke gently to him. Rachel couldn't hear what she said, but Shadow was suddenly happy to take the bit.

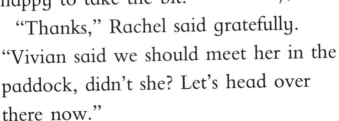

"Thanks," Rachel said gratefully. "Vivian said we should meet her in the paddock, didn't she? Let's head over there now."

The girls led their ponies through the
stable yard and out to the paddock,
but, when they arrived, they were
surprised to see a boy already there
on a grey horse. He was cantering
in a circle, riding confidently and with
skill – he was certainly having much
more success than anyone else they'd
seen that day.

The girls stopped and watched closely. As the grey horse jumped over a brush box, the boy's hard hat lifted up ever so slightly. Kirsty gasped; the movement of the boy's hat had just revealed a pointy green nose!

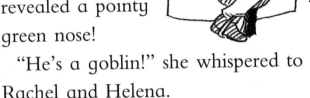

"He's a goblin!" she whispered to Rachel and Helena.

"And he's wearing my hat!" Helena exclaimed crossly.

Rachel frowned. "But it's so big," she said. "The hat, I mean. I was expecting it to be the same size as it was in Fairyland."

"No," Helena said. "You see, the Magic Sporty Objects adjust their size to suit whoever is holding them."

"So how are we going to get it back?" Kirsty wondered. "If the goblin sees us coming after his hat, he'll just ride away."

Rachel thought hard. "Helena, what do horses like to eat more than anything else?" she asked.

"Most horses love sugar lumps," the little fairy replied. "Why?"

Rachel smiled. "Could you use your magic to conjure some up?" she asked.

Helena nodded. "Of course," she said, waving her wand.

Immediately,
a pile of sparkling
white sugar cubes
appeared in
Rachel's hand.

"Great!" Rachel declared. "Now, how about we try tempting that horse over to us with a trail of sugar lumps? Then we might be able to persuade the goblin to give us back the hat!"

"Good idea," said Kirsty.

Helena waved her wand again, and a flurry of horseshoe-shaped fairy dust swirled all around the pile of sugar lumps. Then, one by one, the cubes jumped down from Rachel's hand and started bouncing along the grass, lining up to make a trail from the girls towards the horse.

It didn't take long for the grey horse to spot the sugar lumps. She had been cantering but she slowed at the sight of her favourite snack, and immediately dipped her head to eat one of the sugar lumps.

The goblin seemed a little confused at the appearance of the sugar, and he looked around. Then he noticed the girls in the corner of the paddock, and frowned. "What are you doing here?"

he asked. Then a suspicious look came over his face and he touched the hat protectively. "Hey — you haven't seen any fairies around here, have you?"

Rachel and Kirsty exchanged glances and gulped. How were they going to answer that question truthfully without scaring the goblin away?

A Ride to the Rescue

Rachel thought quickly. "Fairies? I can't see any fairies," she replied, and it was quite true – since Helena was now hiding at the bottom of Kirsty's pocket.

"That hat you're wearing…" Kirsty said to the goblin as the grey horse came nearer, eating the next sugar lump in the line. "It's not yours, is it?"

The goblin gave a crafty smile. "No, but I'm keeping it," he told her, and winked. "This hat is going to help my team win at the Fairyland Olympics!"

"But that would be cheating," Rachel said. "Listen... If you give it back to us, we can return it to its rightful owner."

The goblin cackled and shook his head. "Not likely," he said. "It's mine now. Oh, I'll show those fairies a thing or – Hey!" He broke off in surprise as

Helena shot out of Kirsty's pocket and zoomed towards him, a determined look on her face. "Oi! What are you doing?" the goblin cried as she flew towards the hat. She pushed at it with her tiny hands, but, unfortunately, she was too small and she couldn't move it one bit.

"Oh, no, you don't!" the goblin yelled. He batted Helena away, tugged on his horse's reins, and cantered off, leaving the fairy fluttering in his wake.

"You can't catch me!" he yelled gleefully over his shoulder.

Rachel and Kirsty ran over to their own ponies, mounted them quickly and urged them to chase after the goblin. Helena flew alongside. "Try to stay as close to the goblin as you can," she encouraged them. "While you're near my Magic Hard Hat, its power will affect you, too, so you'll be able to ride well."

"OK," Kirsty replied, hunching lower over Brandy and urging him to go faster.

56

"But it works both ways," Helena added. "The further you are from the hat, the worse your riding will become."

"Come on, Shadow," Rachel urged. "Keep going!"

The girls gradually gained ground on the goblin and soon realised that Helena was right. The nearer they got to him, the easier it was to ride.

But then the goblin glanced over his shoulder and looked panicked to see how close the girls were getting. He urged his horse on and it broke into a gallop, pulling away from Brandy and Shadow.

As the gap widened, Kirsty could feel her control slipping. Brandy stumbled on a tufty bit of grass, and slowed nervously.

Rachel, too, was struggling to stay in her saddle, but she knew they had to get closer to the goblin's horse again. "Come on, boy," she said encouragingly. "You can do it!"

All three of them were now approaching a tall hedge that bordered the paddock. It was a huge jump, but the goblin's horse didn't hesitate and took it at full speed. Thanks to the magic of the hard hat, the horse cleared the hedge easily, leaving the girls behind on the other side.

With the tall hedge now between them, the effect of the Magic Hard Hat wore off completely, and Rachel bumped horribly on Shadow's back.

Kirsty, too, was being jolted around, and felt very frightened. She was getting closer and closer to the hedge, which looked more enormous by the second. She wasn't at all confident that Brandy was going to be able to jump high enough, not when her riding skills seemed to have vanished. She tried frantically to think of a way to stop her pony, but her mind was blank with fright. She couldn't remember what to do!

Kirsty glanced over at Rachel, wondering if her friend could help, but Rachel looked just as terrified. She was white-faced, clinging on to Shadow for dear life as he thundered towards the hedge.

Kirsty's hands were sweating, and suddenly the reins slipped from her grasp altogether. "Help!" she cried, as she felt herself falling…

Helena Helps

Just as Kirsty thought she was about to hit the ground, there was a flash of bright pink light in her eyes, and she felt herself shrinking. Down, down, down she went, smaller and smaller, until she was a fairy with shining fairy wings. She fluttered her wings thankfully and soared into the air.

Rachel was doing the same, and both girls flew gratefully over to Helena. "Thank you," gasped Rachel. "That was scary!"

Brandy and Shadow both jumped over the hedge without their riders, and then came to a stop in the next field, putting their heads down to graze.

Seeing that their ponies were safe, the three fairies zoomed after the goblin, whose horse was still galloping.

"We've got to think of a way to get that hat off his head," Rachel said as they flew. "But how?"

"Helena, could your magic undo the strap?" Kirsty wondered. Helena nodded, and Kirsty pointed towards a jump the goblin's horse was now approaching. "If we can catch up with him in time, maybe you could magic the buckle undone just after the jump," she said. "Then, as his horse lands, the hat should fly off his head..."

"And we can catch it!" Rachel finished.

"Brilliant idea," Helena said warmly. "Let's do it!"

The three fairies flew on towards the goblin. "Of course, once the hat comes off his head, he won't be able to ride very well any more," Helena murmured to herself, "so I'll have to make sure he's all right."

"He's coming up to the jump!" Rachel cried.

Helena pointed her wand at the Magic Hard Hat. As the goblin's horse rose up to meet the fence, a swirling cloud of pink fairy dust fluttered in the air. As the goblin landed on the other side, the strap slid smoothly through the buckle and came undone – and the hat lifted, too, straight off the goblin's head!

As the hat flew through the air, Rachel and Kirsty darted towards it and caught it between them. Immediately, the hat shimmered and then shrank down to its Fairyland size.

Meanwhile, the goblin had completely lost control of his horse and had bounced right out of the saddle.

"Whoaaaa!" he cried in alarm as he tumbled towards the ground.

But Helena deftly flicked her wand at a nearby water trough, which whizzed through the air and stopped just under the tumbling goblin. He fell into the water with a mighty *splash!* Kirsty and Rachel couldn't help chuckling. They knew goblins hated getting wet. "It serves him right, for trying to cheat," Rachel said, as the goblin clambered out of the trough, dripping wet.

"Maybe you should go back to Fairyland and dry off!" Helena called as he stomped off in a huff.

Kirsty and Rachel gave the Magic Hard
Hat to Helena, who popped it back on
her head with a smile of relief.

"Thank you," she said,
and touched her
wand to it. There
was a flash of
twinkling pink lights
all around the hat.

"There," she said happily. "I've just
set everything to rights. Horseriding
is a lot more safe and fun again for
everyone!"

"Hurrah!" cheered Rachel and Kirsty.

Helena gave them both a hug, then
waved her wand to turn them back to
their normal sizes. "Thanks again, girls,"
she said. "I'll fly to Fairyland now and
tell the others the good news!"

"Bye, Helena,"
Kirsty said,
waving as she
and Rachel
watched the little
fairy zoom away.

"Oh, girls, there you are! And you've
found Mischief, well done!" came
a voice, and Vivian strode into
the paddock.

Rachel and Kirsty looked at each other, realising that Mischief must be the name of the grey horse the goblin had been riding. "Yes, she was in the paddock," Rachel said truthfully. "We followed her here."

Vivian looked very relieved. "Thank goodness," she said. "She must have got loose in all the turmoil. Thank you, girls. I'll take her back to the stables, then we can begin your lesson. I'm sorry for the slow start today, but everything seems to be back to normal in the yard now."

Kirsty and Rachel smiled at each other. They knew why everything was

back to normal. It was because Helena
the Horseriding Fairy had her Magic
Hard Hat back again.

"That was exciting," Rachel said,
as she mounted Shadow, noticing
how much easier it was this time.

Kirsty nodded. "Yes," she said. "Now we just have to find the other six Magic Sporty Objects in time for the Fairyland Olympics." She grinned. "I think this is going to be a *fairy* busy week!"

Now Rachel and Kirsty
must help...

Francesca the Football Fairy

Read on for a sneak peek...

"You look great, Dad!" Rachel Walker laughed, glancing at her father as she climbed out of the car. Mr Walker was wearing a blue and white football shirt and scarf, his face was painted with blue and white stripes, and he had a fluffy blue and white wig on his head.

"The wig's fantastic!" Kirsty Tate, Rachel's best friend, added with a grin. She was staying with the Walkers over the spring holiday. "He's going to be the best-dressed Tippington Rovers supporter here."

Rachel nodded. "I'm glad Mum and I are just wearing scarves, though," she added. "That wig looks a bit hot!"

"It is, but I want to show my support for the team," said Mr Walker, as they left the car park and joined the other football fans heading towards the Cooke Stadium. "This is a very important match, girls. If Tippington beat Alton United today, the team will be promoted to the next league!"

Rachel and Kirsty exchanged concerned glances.

They were both worried that the football match would be a complete disaster, because the Sporty Fairies had lost their Magic Sporty Objects. When these special objects were in their proper places, with the Sporty Fairies or in the fairies' lockers, they made sure that sport in both the human and fairy worlds was safe, fun and exciting. Unfortunately, they'd been stolen by cunning Jack Frost and his goblin servants...

Read Francesca the Football Fairy to find out what adventures are in store for Kirsty and Rachel!

Meet the
Friendship Fairies

When Jack Frost steals the Friendship Fairies' magical objects, BFFs everywhere are in trouble! Can Rachel and Kirsty help save the magic of friendship?

www.rainbowmagicbooks.co.uk

RAINBOW magic

Calling all parents, carers and teachers!
The Rainbow Magic fairies are here to help
your child enter the magical world of reading.
Whatever reading stage they are at, there's
a Rainbow Magic book for everyone!
Here is Lydia the Reading Fairy's guide to
supporting your child's journey at all levels.

Starting Out

Our Rainbow Magic Beginner Readers are perfect for first-time readers who are just beginning to develop reading skills and confidence. Approved by teachers, they contain a full range of educational levelling, as well as lively full-colour illustrations.

Developing Readers

Rainbow Magic Early Readers contain longer stories and wider vocabulary for building stamina and growing confidence. These are adaptations of our most popular Rainbow Magic stories, specially developed for younger readers in conjunction with an Early Years reading consultant, with full-colour illustrations.

Going Solo

The Rainbow Magic chapter books - a mixture of series and one-off specials - contain accessible writing to encourage your child to venture into reading independently. These highly collectible and much-loved magical stories inspire a love of reading to last a lifetime.

www.rainbowmagicbooks.co.uk

"Rainbow Magic got my daughter reading chapter books. Great sparkly covers, cute fairies and traditional stories full of magic that she found impossible to put down" - Mother of Edie (6 years)

"Florence LOVES the Rainbow Magic books. She really enjoys reading now" - Mother of Florence (6 years)

The Rainbow Magic Reading Challenge

Well done, fairy friend – you have completed the book!
This book was worth 5 points.

See how far you have climbed on the
Reading Rainbow opposite.

The more books you read, the more points you will get,
and the closer you will be to becoming a Fairy Princess!

How to get your Reading Rainbow
1. Cut out the coin below
2. Go to the Rainbow Magic website
3. Download and print out your poster
4. Add your coin and climb up the Reading Rainbow!

There's all this and lots more at
www.rainbowmagicbooks.co.uk

You'll find activities, competitions, stories, a special
newsletter and complete profiles of all the
Rainbow Magic fairies. Find a fairy with your name!

The Sporty Fairies

Special thanks to
Narinder Dhami

ORCHARD BOOKS

First published in Great Britain in 2008 by
Orchard Books
This edition published in 2017 by
The Watts Publishing Group

1 3 5 7 9 10 8 6 4 2

HIT entertainment

Copyright © 2008 Rainbow Magic Limited.
Copyright © 2008 HIT Entertainment Limited.
Illustrations copyright © Orchard Books, 2008

A CIP catalogue record for this book is available from the British Library.

ISBN 978 1 40835 322 6

Printed in Great Britain by Clays Ltd, St Ives plc

MIX
Paper from
responsible sources
FSC® C104740

The paper and board used in this book are made from wood from responsible sources

Orchard Books
An imprint of Hachette Children's Group
Part of The Watts Publishing Group Limited
Carmelite House, 50 Victoria Embankment, London EC4Y 0DZ

An Hachette UK Company
www.hachette.co.uk
www.hachettechildrens.co.uk

Francesca
the Football
Fairy

by Daisy Meadows

Join the Rainbow Magic Reading Challenge!

Read the story and collect your fairy points to climb the
Reading Rainbow at the back of the book.

This book is worth 5 points.

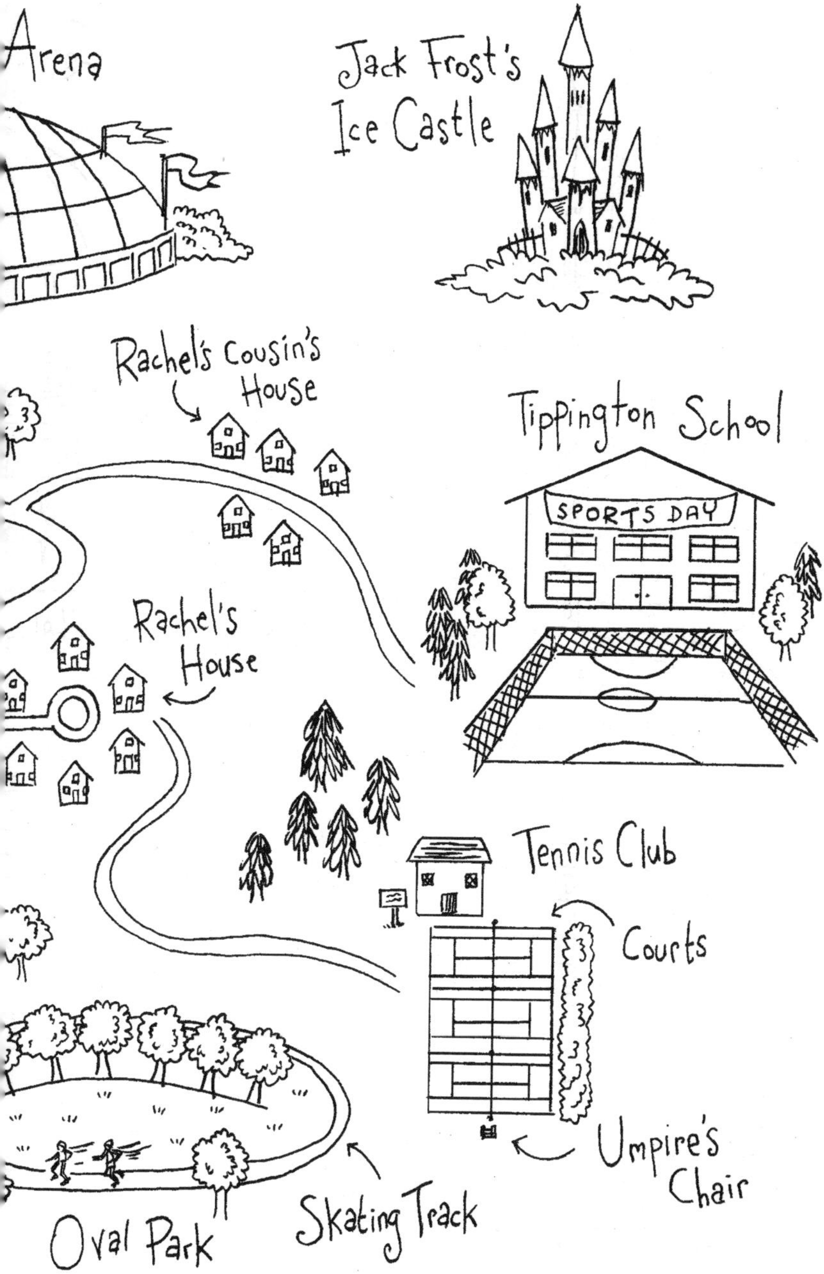

Arena

Jack Frost's
Ice Castle

Rachel's Cousin's
House

Tippington School

SPORTS DAY

Rachel's
House

Tennis Club

Courts

Oval Park

Skating Track

Umpire's
Chair

The Fairyland Olympics are about to start,
And my expert goblins are going to take part.
We will win this year, for I've got a cunning plan.
I'm sending my goblins to the arena in Fairyland.

The Magic Sporty Objects that make sports safe and fun,
Will be stolen by my goblins, to keep until we've won.
Sporty Fairies, prepare to lose and to watch us win.
Goblins, follow my commands, and let the games begin!

Contents

Football Fun

"You look great, Dad!" Rachel Walker laughed, glancing at her father as she climbed out of the car. Mr Walker was wearing a blue and white football shirt and scarf, his face was painted with blue and white stripes, and he had a fluffy blue and white wig on his head.

"The wig's fantastic!" Kirsty Tate, Rachel's best friend, added with a grin. She was staying with the Walkers over the spring holiday. "He's going to be the best-dressed Tippington Rovers supporter here."

Rachel nodded. "I'm glad Mum and I are just wearing scarves, though," she added. "That wig looks a bit hot!"

"It is, but I want to show my support for the team," said Mr Walker, as they left the car park and joined the other football fans heading towards the Cooke Stadium. "This is a very important match, girls. If Tippington beat Alton United today, the team will be promoted to the next league!"

Rachel and Kirsty exchanged concerned glances. They were both worried that the football match would be a complete disaster, because the Sporty Fairies had lost their Magic Sporty Objects.

When these special objects were in their
proper places, with the Sporty Fairies
or in the fairies' lockers, they made
sure that sport in both the human
and fairy worlds was safe, fun and
exciting. Unfortunately, they'd been
stolen by cunning Jack Frost and his
goblin servants.

Jack Frost was determined to win the
Fairyland Olympics, which started in
six days' time, and so he'd ordered
his goblins to hide the objects away
in the human world until the games
took place. Then, by keeping the
Magic Sporty Objects close to them,
the goblins would win every single
event. The Fairyland Olympics couldn't
be cancelled because that would ruin
the Olympic Games in the human

world, so Rachel and Kirsty had promised their fairy friends that they would do their best to find the objects before the games took place.

"I'm glad we persuaded Mum and Dad to come to the match early today," Rachel said quietly to Kirsty. "Maybe the goblin who has Francesca the Football Fairy's Magic Football will be here, too."

"Helena the Horseriding Fairy did say that any goblin who has one of the magic objects will be near that sport," Kirsty agreed.

The girls had helped Helena to get her Magic Hard Hat back just the day before. "She said that Jack Frost has told the goblins to practise their sporty skills before the Fairyland Olympics, remember?"

"Yes, and King Oberon said that the winning Olympic team will get the Fairyland Olympics Cup, which is filled with luck," Kirsty reminded Rachel. "Think how much more mischief Jack Frost could cause if he had loads of good luck!"

"Girls, come and have your picture taken," called Mrs Walker, holding up her camera.

"Ooh, good idea," Rachel said, as she and Kirsty hurried over to join her parents outside the stadium entrance.

"Then we won't forget how much effort Dad's put into his outfit!"

"I feel like the odd one out," Kirsty joked, as Mrs Walker took their photo. "I'm the only one without any Tippington Rovers colours on."

"There's a kiosk inside the stadium that sells merchandise," Rachel's dad told her. "We'll buy you a scarf there."

"Thank you!" Kirsty exclaimed.

As they went inside the stadium, Rachel immediately started looking around for any sign of goblins, but she didn't see any flashes of goblin green.

Remember, you have to let the magic come to you, Rachel told herself. But she couldn't help hoping that the magic came before the match started, otherwise the game would be ruined.

There weren't many people inside the stadium yet, so there was no queue at the merchandise kiosk. They headed straight over to it, and Mr Walker bought a scarf for Kirsty.

"Here you are, dear," said the shop assistant, popping the scarf into a carrier bag and handing it to Kirsty. "Enjoy the game."

"Thank you," Kirsty said gratefully.

"Let's go and find our seats,"
Mrs Walker suggested.

They all went into the main part
of the stadium, which was still fairly
empty. Kirsty and Rachel had the
chance to take a good look around,
but neither of the girls could see
anything out of the ordinary.

"Maybe we should explore," Kirsty

whispered to Rachel. "There may be goblin mischief going on somewhere else."

"Dad, is it OK if Kirsty and I go and look around?" asked Rachel.

"That's fine," Mr Walker replied, settling himself in his seat. "We'll sit and watch the pre-match build-up on the giant TV screens."

"Just make sure you're back before the match starts," Rachel's mum added.

The girls nodded.

"I'll put my new scarf on," Kirsty said, as she and Rachel hurried off.

She opened the bag, and a cloud of glittering sparkles immediately burst from inside. Then, as both girls stared in surprise, the scarf snaked gracefully out of the bag, with a tiny fairy perched daintily on the end of it!

Commentary Confusion

"It's Francesca the Football Fairy!"
Kirsty cried in delight.

"Hello, girls!" Francesca called. She
wore a green and yellow football shirt
with matching shorts and football boots,
and her long hair was braided and tied
back in a ponytail. She hovered in the
air in front of the girls as the scarf

settled around Kirsty's neck. "I have
a feeling those very unsporting goblins
may be here!" she added.

"We've been looking out for them,"
Rachel told her, "but we haven't seen
any yet…"

Suddenly, one of the stadium officials
came running towards them. Francesca
quickly hid behind a fold of Kirsty's scarf,
but the official was too busy speaking
into a walkie-talkie to notice her.

"Yes, all the footballs in the stadium have vanished!" he exclaimed. "If we don't find one – and soon – the game will have to be cancelled!" And, with that, he disappeared into the players' tunnel.

"Hmm. Missing footballs! This has goblin mischief written all over it," Francesca said.

"But why would a goblin have taken all the footballs?" asked Rachel, puzzled.

"Yes, if he's got your Magic Football, why would he need any others?" Kirsty asked.

"I don't know," Francesca replied.

"Well, let's see if we can find the goblin and get the footballs back," Rachel suggested.

Just then, Kirsty's attention was caught by one of the giant TV screens overhead. "Rachel, look," she cried. "There's your dad!"

Rachel glanced up and her face broke into a grin. Mr Walker was on the TV screen, being interviewed by a football commentator.

"So, Mr Walker, what do you think will happen in the game today?" asked the commentator.

"Oh, Tippington Rovers will win!" Rachel's dad replied confidently. "I think the score will be two-nil."

"I like your dad's wig, Rachel!" Francesca chuckled.

The commentator thanked Mr Walker, turned away and headed through the stadium, still talking to the camera.

"OK, girls," Francesca said. "Where shall we look for goblins?"

Just as Kirsty was about to look away from the TV screen, the commentator opened the door of his commentary box and she saw that there was someone inside. A small person wearing a tracksuit, a Tippington Rovers woolly hat and a red Alton United scarf was sitting on the floor, rummaging through a big net filled with footballs.

"Oh, hello," said the commentator, sounding surprised. "Are you here to cover the match with me?"

25

Curiously, Kirsty stared up at the screen, wondering why all the footballs were hidden away in the commentary box.

The small man looked up irritably at the commentator's words. As he did so, the scarf, which was wrapped around the bottom of his face, slipped, and Kirsty caught a glimpse of green.

"Oh!" she gasped, "There's the goblin!"

"Where?" Rachel and Francesca both said together, looking around.

"Up there," Kirsty told them, pointing at the TV. "He's in the commentary box with all the footballs!"

As Rachel and Francesca glanced up at the screen, the goblin pulled his scarf quickly back into place, but not before Rachel had spotted a green, pointy nose.

"It is the goblin," she agreed. "And the silly thing's wearing both Tippington and Alton colours!"

"Let's head for the commentary box right away," Francesca called, already zooming into the air. "If the goblin's there, then I bet my Magic Football is too!"

Footballs Galore

Francesca and the girls rushed over to the commentary box. Although they couldn't keep their eyes on the TV screens as they ran, the stadium's loudspeaker system meant that they could hear the commentator still trying to talk to the goblin.

"So, Mr...er..." said the commentator,

sounding confused. "Did you say what your name was?"

"No," the goblin snapped rudely.

"Well, who do you think is going to win the match?" the commentator asked.

"Um…" There was a long silence. "…Manchester United?" the goblin said hesitantly.

Francesca, Rachel and Kirsty couldn't help laughing.

"Manchester United aren't even playing today!" the commentator said crossly.

"Well, that was a silly question anyway," the goblin declared with a loud sniff.

"The commentary box is just around the corner," Rachel panted, pointing at a sign on the wall.

Soon the girls were at the bottom of a flight of stairs that led up to the back of the commentary box. Luckily there was nobody else around.

"What do we do now?" asked Kirsty.

They were near another of the giant TV screens and Rachel glanced up at it.

COMMENTARY BOX

The commentator was spluttering, "Right, and, er...now back to the studio!" Meanwhile, the goblin flung the door of the commentary box open and began to stomp out, dragging the net of footballs behind him.

"The goblin's coming out!" Rachel exclaimed, pointing to the top of the stairs.

The girls started up the steps. They saw the goblin appear above them with the net of footballs.

"STOP RIGHT THERE!"
Francesca shouted.

Startled, the goblin
jumped and let go
of the net. All
the footballs
tumbled out of it,
bouncing down
the steps towards
the girls.

"It's raining
footballs!" Rachel
gasped, trying to
dodge the balls.

"Look out for
Francesca's football,
Rachel!" Kirsty called,
also dodging from side
to side.

"That's fancy footwork, girls!"
Francesca called approvingly
as Kirsty and Rachel
side-stepped the
flying footballs.
The goblin was
rushing down
the steps towards
them now, trying
to gather the
footballs up
in his arms.
Then Rachel
noticed that one
of the footballs
heading straight
towards her was
surrounded by
tiny golden sparkles.

Francesca's Magic Football! Rachel thought, her heart pounding with excitement. She reached out for the special ball, but the goblin had noticed it at exactly the same moment. He dropped the other balls immediately and raced after Francesca's football.

"Get out of my way!" the goblin yelled, shoving Rachel aside. She stumbled, and the Magic Football

bounced past her. The goblin grabbed wildly at it, but missed.

The football bounced to the bottom of the steps, and Rachel and the goblin both raced after it. But, at that very moment, one of the stadium officials came around the corner. He spotted the Magic Football and instantly scooped it up into his arms.

So Near and
Yet So Far

"Oh, no!" Rachel breathed,
dismayed. She glanced at her
fairy friend.

Luckily, Francesca had managed
to whizz out of sight as soon as
the official appeared, and she was
now peeping anxiously out from
behind a lock of Kirsty's hair.

"What's going on here?" the official said sternly, staring at the goblin. "We've been looking for these footballs everywhere. A ballboy is supposed to look after the balls, not lose them!"

The official thinks the goblin is a ballboy! Rachel realised. *The outfit he's wearing must be one of the official ballboy tracksuits.*

⚽ 40 ⚽

"Pick all these footballs up, please," the official went on.

Scowling, the goblin did as he was told, shoving the footballs back into the net one by one. Rachel and Kirsty began to help. *Maybe we'll still have a chance to get the Magic Football back,* Kirsty thought hopefully.

"Oh, don't bother with that, girls," the official said with a smile. "The match will be starting soon, and you don't want to miss it. Off you go."

Reluctantly, Rachel and Kirsty moved away. They watched as the official put the Magic Football into the net with the others. Then he took the net from the goblin and strode off down a corridor which led into the back of the stadium.

"Come on," he said to the goblin,

"We need to find the other ballboys and girls."

The goblin smirked widely at Kirsty and Rachel before skipping off after the official.

"Oh dear," Francesca flew out from behind Kirsty's hair, looking very glum. "Where's he taking my football? We have to get it back!"

"That's going to be difficult," Kirsty said with a frown. She pointed at a sign on the wall of the corridor which read: PRIVATE – NO ACCESS TO THE PUBLIC. "We won't be allowed into the official areas of the stadium. The goblin's only allowed in because that man thinks he's a ballboy."

Francesca winked at her. "Well, with

a little bit of magic, anything's possible. Maybe they could use two more ballgirls…" She waved her wand and then, in a shower of dazzling fairy dust, Kirsty and  Rachel's outfits changed. Now they were both wearing dark blue tracksuits, exactly like the goblin's.

"Let's go!" Rachel cried.

The three friends hurried down the passageway. They couldn't see the goblin or the official, so they began checking the rooms along the corridor. They peeped inside them, but there was no sign of the goblin or the footballs.

Then, as they got towards the corner of the corridor, they heard voices coming from a room with its door ajar.

Rachel and Kirsty peeped around the door. Inside was a large group of ballboys and ballgirls. Each of them was holding a football, and they were listening intently to a man at the front of the room.

"...And remember, it's important to get

the ball back into play as soon
as possible," the man was saying.

Kirsty nudged Rachel. "There's
the net that held the footballs," she
whispered, pointing at the net which
was now lying on the floor, empty.

"But where's Francesca's Magic
Football?" Rachel whispered back,
scanning all the balls in the room for

the tell-tale sparkle of fairy magic. "Nobody in here seems to have it."

"The goblin's not here either," Francesca said with a frown. "He must have got away with my football."

"We'd better go," Kirsty murmured, "otherwise that official might see us and call us into the meeting."

The girls slipped quietly away down the corridor.

"But where shall we start looking for the goblin now?" asked Rachel.

The girls stared at each other in desperation. But, all of a sudden, they heard a croaky voice singing a football chant:

"Go, goblins, go!
  Boot it high,
  Boot it low.

Win, goblins, win!
 Stamp their toes,
 Kick their shins."

"It's the goblin!" Francesca cried.

Football Fever

"After him!" Kirsty shouted.

Francesca and the girls darted around the corner of the corridor. Ahead of them they saw the goblin, still singing croakily to himself. He was running along and expertly dribbling a football ahead of him, occasionally flicking the ball up with his toe and heading it forwards.

"Wow!" Rachel panted as they chased after him. "He's better than some of the Tippington Rovers players!"

"That's the magic of my football at work," Francesca told her.

"Even dribbling that football, he's getting away from us," Kirsty pointed out as the goblin headed towards a door at the bottom of the corridor.

"Girls, you'll be much quicker if you're fairy-sized." Francesca said, raising her wand.

Rachel and Kirsty skidded to a halt, and Francesca showered them with fairy dust. They instantly shrank to become tiny fairies, with glittering wings on their backs.

As Francesca and the girls flew swiftly down the corridor together, the goblin flung the door open and skipped outside, not even bothering to close the door behind him again.

A moment later, Francesca, Kirsty and Rachel reached the door and peeked outside. "Oh, it's the stadium car park!" Rachel exclaimed.

"But where's the goblin?" asked Kirsty, staring at all the coaches and cars parked in neat rows. Lots more football fans were arriving now, too, as it was getting close to the start of the match.

"He must be somewhere in the car park," Francesca decided. "We'll have to search for him, but we mustn't let anyone see us."

Rachel and Kirsty nodded and followed Francesca high up into the air. They hovered above the car park so that they could get a good view of everything below them, but they could see no sign of the goblin anywhere.

"Maybe we should split up and search each part of the car park more carefully," Kirsty suggested.

Rachel was about to reply when her attention was caught by a rather strange sight. A coach was heading very slowly towards one of the car park exits, zig-zagging from side to side.

"Look at that coach," Rachel said to her friends. "Why is it leaving before the match has even started?"

"That *is* odd," Francesca agreed.

"Let's check it out," Kirsty suggested, zooming downwards.

Rachel and Francesca followed. As the three of them drew level with the coach, they peeped in through the windows.

"It's full of goblins!" Kirsty cried, looking up and down the packed coach.

"What are they doing here?" asked Rachel anxiously.

"It's the Goblin Olympic Football Team," Francesca explained, looking worried. "They must be hoping to practise with my Magic Football."

The goblins were dressed in a white football strip which had a picture of Jack Frost on the front. They all looked extremely pleased with themselves, bouncing up and down in their seats and singing loudly:

"Go, goblins, go!
Boot it high,
Boot it low.

Win, goblins, win!
Stamp their toes,
Kick their shins."

"They're not very sporting, are they?" Francesca said, frowning. "'Kick their shins', indeed!"

"But where's the goblin with the Magic Football?" asked Kirsty.

Rachel soon spotted him. The goblin they'd been chasing was now driving the coach, his face screwed up in concentration.

"Look, girls," Francesca whispered, pointing her wand at the goblins' feet. Rachel and Kirsty glanced down and saw the Magic Football rolling around on the floor of the coach.

"Let's go and find somewhere else to practise our football skills," shouted the goblin driver to the rest of the team.

"We've wasted loads of time, though," moaned a goblin at the back of the coach. "Just because you got the Magic Football muddled up with a lot of the humans' footballs."

"Well, I found it again, didn't I?" the goblin at the wheel retorted. "Anyway, I was just checking out the stadium to find somewhere for us to practise. I didn't know some silly humans were going to be playing a match here today!"

"Can't you go any faster?" demanded another goblin.

"Yes, at this rate we won't have left the car park before the Fairyland Olympics start in six days!" another added.

"Shut up!" the goblin at the wheel snapped crossly. "We've got the Magic Football, and that's all that matters. Those pesky fairies won't stand a chance of beating us at the Fairyland Olympics!"

The goblins cheered loudly. Meanwhile, Francesca, Rachel and Kirsty looked at each other in concern.

"How are we going to get the Magic
Football back?" Kirsty whispered as they
hovered beside the slow-moving coach.
"There are just too many goblins around!"

Rachel thought for a moment. "Maybe
we can distract the driver while Francesca
sneaks onto the coach and gets her football
back," she suggested.

"Good idea," Francesca agreed. "When
I try to pick the ball up, it will
immediately shrink to its Fairyland size,
but it's going to be difficult for me to get
close to it while it's rolling around on
the floor. You'll have to try to buy me
as much time as you can, girls."

"We will!" Kirsty said in a determined
voice.

Francesca pointed her wand at the
driver's window and, with a few sparkles

of fairy magic, it slid open a crack.

"Good luck, girls," Francesca whispered as the three of them zipped in quickly through the open window.

Kirsty and Rachel both felt very nervous as they watched Francesca zoom down towards the football. Would their plan work?

Goblins, Go Home!

"Let's give this goblin a surprise, Kirsty," Rachel whispered.

Kirsty nodded, and followed Rachel down to land on the top of the steering-wheel.

"Hello!" Rachel called, waving up at the goblin.

"Remember us?" Kirsty added.

The goblin's eyes almost popped out of his head. "Are you girls or fairies?" he asked, scratching his head in confusion. Then he let out a squeal of rage. "Ooh, you're both!" And he took his hands off the steering-wheel and began swiping furiously at the girls.

As Rachel and Kirsty dodged out of his way, the coach began to swerve wildly. Kirsty glanced down and saw that the Magic Football was rolling about all over the place. Francesca just couldn't get close to it at all.

"Look out!" Rachel gasped suddenly, as she saw the coach heading straight towards a row of parked cars.

"Hit the brakes!" Kirsty shouted.

Looking scared, the goblin slammed on the brakes. The coach shuddered to a halt, just nudging one of the cars ever so gently on its bumper. Rachel, Kirsty and the goblins breathed sighs of relief.

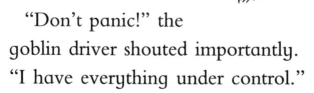

"Don't panic!" the goblin driver shouted importantly. "I have everything under control."

But, at that very moment, the airbag inside the steering-wheel inflated. It ballooned out and completely muffled the goblin's head.

"Help!" spluttered the goblin. "I've been attacked by a giant balloon!"

But, instead of rushing to help their friend, the other goblins on the coach roared with laughter. Rachel and Kirsty grinned at each other, then glanced down at Francesca. Now that the coach had stopped, she was able to reach her Magic Football, and shrank it quickly to its Fairyland size.

Beaming all over her face, Francesca scooped up her precious football and then zoomed upwards to join Rachel and Kirsty. "Thanks, girls," Francesca laughed. "Now, let's get out of here."

The three of them whizzed out of the open window again, just as the driver-goblin managed to struggle free of the airbag. He glanced down and scowled when he saw that the football had gone.

"Those fairies have stolen the Magic Football!" he shouted.

Immediately, the goblins scrambled off the coach as quickly as they could to race after Francesca and the girls. The three fairies hovered in mid-air, just out of reach.

"You goblins had better go home and start practising your football skills," Francesca said sternly, "because you won't have the Magic Football to help you now!"

The goblins moaned and grumbled when they saw the sparkling football tucked safely under Francesca's arm.

"Why didn't you stop them taking the football?" shouted the driver-goblin to his friends.

"Don't blame us!" the other goblins muttered. "This is all your fault!"

"Off you go, back to Fairyland," said Francesca.

The goblins muttered grumpily and stuck out their tongues at Francesca and the girls, but they stomped off.

"They've got a lot of football practice to do now," Francesca said with a grin.

"But if they do win at the fairy games, at least they'll have won fair and square. And now I must go straight back to Fairyland and tell everyone the good news, but first, there are a few things I must put right..."

Francesca touched the Magic Football with her wand, and a sparkling burst of 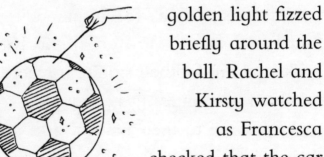 golden light fizzed briefly around the ball. Rachel and Kirsty watched as Francesca checked that the car the coach had bumped into wasn't damaged. Then she pointed her wand at the coach and a burst of fairy dust surrounded it, rolling it gently back into an empty parking space.

Finally, Francesca led Rachel and Kirsty
back into the football stadium, where
another cloud of fairy dust turned
the girls back to their normal sizes and
returned them to their original outfits.

"Thank you again, girls," Francesca
said, her eyes twinkling. "Everything
will be fine with the Tippington and
Alton match now, and it's just about
to start, so go and enjoy yourselves!"

Rachel and Kirsty waved as Francesca shot upwards. "Goodbye," they called.

Francesca waved back and blew the girls a kiss. Then, with a cheeky smile, she began dribbling her Magic Football from toe to toe in mid-air. Next second, she and the football both vanished in a cloud of fairy sparkles.

"We can really enjoy the match, Kirsty," Rachel said happily as they rushed back to their seats, "now that we know Francesca has her football back."

Kirsty grinned and nodded. "Yes, and let's hope Tippington Rovers win," she cheered.

RAINBOW magic

The Sporty Fairies

Rachel and Kirsty must now help

Zoe the Skating Fairy

Jack Frost's scheming goblins have stolen Zoe's Magic Lace and are using it to improve their chances of winning the Fairyland Olympics! Can Rachel and Kirsty help Zoe to get it back?

Skating Struggles

Rachel Walker held on tightly to the park railings as she stood up on her in-line skates. "Whoa-a-a!" she laughed, as her feet moved slightly in different directions. "How are you getting on, Kirsty?"

Kirsty Tate, Rachel's best friend, was still sitting on the grass, tying the laces on her skates. She fastened the top straps, then smiled up at Rachel. Kirsty was staying with Rachel's family for a week during the Easter holidays, and today the girls had come to Oval Park, near the Walkers' house.

"All right…I think," Kirsty replied,
clutching Rachel's hand and standing up.
Then she grinned. "We must be mad to
be skating today after everything that's
happened to the Sporty Fairies," she said,
wobbling on her wheels.

"At least we're well-protected," Rachel
reminded her, tapping on Kirsty's helmet.
"And this is such a good place to skate,
I'm sure we'll still have fun."

The girls certainly were well-protected
– with helmets, knee pads and elbow
pads, just in case either of them took
a tumble. And Rachel was right, the park
was perfect for skating, with its wide path
looping around the edge, where lots of
skaters and skateboarders were trying out
their skills. It was a warm sunny day,
with a fresh breeze just rustling through

the leaves in the trees, and making the daffodils nod their yellow heads.

Unfortunately, there seemed to be a lot of bumps and falls taking place amongst the skaters today. This was because Zoe the Skating Fairy's Magic Lace was missing. That meant skaters and skateboarders everywhere were having trouble...

Read the rest of

Zoe the Skating Fairy

to find out what magic happens next...

RAINBOW magic

Calling all parents, carers and teachers!
The Rainbow Magic fairies are here to help
your child enter the magical world of reading.
Whatever reading stage they are at, there's
a Rainbow Magic book for everyone!
Here is Lydia the Reading Fairy's guide to
supporting your child's journey at all levels.

Starting Out

1

Our Rainbow Magic Beginner Readers are perfect for first-time readers who are just beginning to develop reading skills and confidence. Approved by teachers, they contain a full range of educational levelling, as well as lively full-colour illustrations.

Developing Readers

2

Rainbow Magic Early Readers contain longer stories and wider vocabulary for building stamina and growing confidence. These are adaptations of our most popular Rainbow Magic stories, specially developed for younger readers in conjunction with an Early Years reading consultant, with full-colour illustrations.

Going Solo

3

The Rainbow Magic chapter books - a mixture of series and one-off specials - contain accessible writing to encourage your child to venture into reading independently. These highly collectible and much-loved magical stories inspire a love of reading to last a lifetime.

www.rainbowmagicbooks.co.uk

"Rainbow Magic got my daughter reading chapter books. Great sparkly covers, cute fairies and traditional stories full of magic that she found impossible to put down" - Mother of Edie (6 years)

"Florence LOVES the Rainbow Magic books. She really enjoys reading now" - Mother of Florence (6 years)

The Rainbow Magic Reading Challenge

Well done, fairy friend – you have completed the book!
This book was worth 5 points.

See how far you have climbed on the **Reading Rainbow**
on the Rainbow Magic website below.

The more books you read, the more points you will get,
and the closer you will be to becoming a Fairy Princess!

How to get your Reading Rainbow
1. Cut out the coin below
2. Go to the Rainbow Magic website
3. Download and print out your poster
4. Add your coin and climb up the Reading Rainbow!

There's all this and lots more at
www.rainbowmagicbooks.co.uk

You'll find activities, competitions, stories, a special
newsletter and complete profiles of all the
Rainbow Magic fairies. Find a fairy with your name!

The Sporty Fairies

For Aphra O'Brien

Special thanks to
Sue Mongredien

ORCHARD BOOKS

First published in Great Britain in 2008 by
Orchard Books
This edition published in 2017 by
The Watts Publishing Group

1 3 5 7 9 10 8 6 4 2

Copyright © 2008 Rainbow Magic Limited.
Copyright © 2008 HIT Entertainment Limited.   HIT entertainment
Illustrations copyright © Orchard Books, 2008

A CIP catalogue record for this book is available from the British Library.

ISBN 978 1 40835 323 3

Printed in Great Britain by Clays Ltd, St Ives plc

MIX
Paper from
responsible sources
FSC® C104740

The paper and board used in this book are made from wood from responsible sources

Orchard Books
An imprint of Hachette Children's Group
Part of The Watts Publishing Group Limited
Carmelite House, 50 Victoria Embankment, London EC4Y 0DZ

An Hachette UK Company
www.hachette.co.uk
www.hachettechildrens.co.uk

Zoe
the Skating
Fairy

by Daisy Meadows

Join the Rainbow Magic Reading Challenge!

Read the story and collect your fairy points to climb the
Reading Rainbow at the back of the book.

This book is worth 5 points.

The Fairyland Palace

Fairyl

Car Park

Coaches

Cooke Football Stadium

Riding Stable

Netball Courts

Football Pitches

Tippington Town

LEISURE CENTRE

Swimming Pool

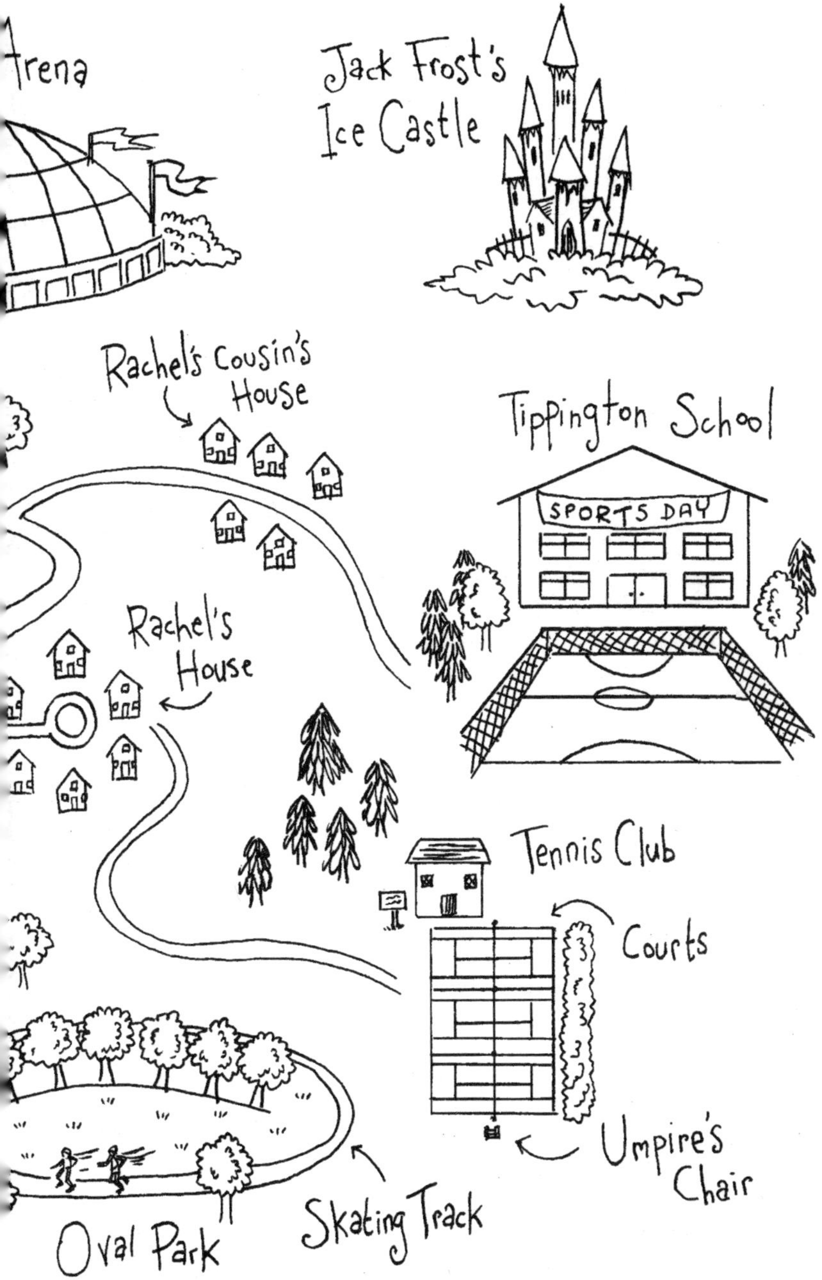

Arena

Jack Frost's
Ice Castle

Rachel's Cousin's
House

Tippington School

SPORTS DAY

Rachel's
House

Tennis Club

Courts

Umpire's
Chair

Oval Park

Skating Track

The Fairyland Olympics are about to start,
And my crafty goblins are going to take part.
We'll win this year, for I've got a cunning plan.
I'm sending my goblins to the arena in Fairyland.

The Magic Sporty Objects that make sports safe and fun,
Will be stolen by my goblins, to keep until we've won.
Sporty Fairies, prepare to lose and to watch us win.
Goblins, follow my commands, and let the games begin!

Contents

Skating Struggles

Rachel Walker held on tightly to the
park railings as she stood up on her
in-line skates. "Whoa-a-a!" she laughed,
as her feet moved slightly in different
directions. "How are you getting
on, Kirsty?"

Kirsty Tate, Rachel's best friend, was
still sitting on the grass, tying the laces

on her skates. She fastened the top straps, then smiled up at Rachel. Kirsty was staying with Rachel's family for a week during the Easter holidays, and today the girls had come to Oval Park, near the Walkers' house.

"All right...I think," Kirsty replied, clutching Rachel's hand and standing up. Then she grinned. "We must be mad to be skating today after everything that's happened to the Sporty Fairies," she said, wobbling on her wheels.

"At least we're well-protected," Rachel reminded her, tapping on Kirsty's helmet. "And this is such a good place to skate, I'm sure we'll still have fun."

The girls certainly were well-protected – with helmets, knee pads and elbow pads, just in case either of them took a tumble. And Rachel was right, the park was perfect for skating, with its wide path looping around the edge, where lots of skaters and skateboarders were trying out their skills. It was a warm sunny day, with a fresh breeze just rustling through the leaves in the trees, and making the daffodils nod their yellow heads.

Unfortunately, there seemed to be a lot of bumps and falls taking place amongst the skaters today. Kirsty and

Rachel watched as a boy on
a skateboard tried to do a jump,
mis-timed it, and fell off
his board onto the
grass nearby. He
got up, unhurt
but looking
puzzled. "Why
isn't that jump
working today?"
they heard him
mutter to himself.

The girls exchanged
glances. They knew why he
was struggling with the jump. It was
because Zoe the Skating Fairy's Magic
Lace was missing. That meant skaters
and skateboarders everywhere were
having trouble.

Nobody else knew it – not even their parents – but Rachel and Kirsty had a wonderful secret. They were friends with the fairies, and had helped them out many times. This time, they had been called to Fairyland by King Oberon and Queen Titania, who'd asked them to help the Sporty Fairies find their Magic Sporty Objects. When the Magic Sporty Objects were in their proper places – either with their fairy keepers, or in their lockers – they ensured that sports were fun and safe for everyone in the human world and in Fairyland. But when the objects weren't where they were supposed to be, their magic only worked on anyone who was very near the object itself.

The Fairyland Olympics were due
to be held soon, and Jack Frost was
desperate to win the prize – a golden cup
full of luck. That was why he'd ordered
his goblins to steal the Magic Sporty
Objects from the fairies' lockers. He
wanted his goblin team to win all
the events, and get the prize.

While the Sporty Fairies were without
their special objects, things were going
wrong in sports all over the world. Kirsty
and Rachel had already helped find
Helena the Horseriding Fairy's Magic
Hard Hat and Francesca the Football
Fairy's Magic Football. But there were
still five Magic Sporty Objects missing.

"I hope we find Zoe's Magic Lace
soon," Rachel said, as she stepped shakily
onto the path and took a step forwards.

14

"I don't feel very confident on these skates today."

Kirsty nodded. "Nor me," she replied. "But remember what the Fairy Queen always says: we mustn't go looking for fairy magic; it will find us!"

The girls set off along the path, leaning forward and swinging their arms to help them skate faster. It was hard work, though, and they kept losing their balance.

"I know I'm usually better at skating than this," Kirsty sighed as she wobbled around a corner.

Whoosh! Just then, four young skaters, wearing identical tracksuits and in-line skates, zipped past the girls at an amazing speed. Rachel and Kirsty almost fell over in surprise.

Rachel stared after them. "Well, they seem to be doing all right," she remarked.

The girls watched the group of skaters, who had now moved into a diamond formation. They looked like young boys but then, as the one at the front turned to call something to the one at the back, Kirsty noticed that he had a greenish tint to his skin.

"They're goblins!" Kirsty gasped.

Rachel nodded. "Yes," she said, "and since they're all skating so well, I bet they've got Zoe's Magic Lace with them!"

An Unexpected Shower

"After them!" cried Kirsty, and she and Rachel did their best to skate faster after the four goblins, but it was no good. The girls were just too slow and shaky, and they could see that there was no way they were going to be able to catch up with the speedy skaters.

"What can we do?" Rachel said helplessly. "The goblins are already way ahead of us."

"And, look, the path bends through the trees further along," Kirsty pointed out. "They'll be out of sight soon."

The girls rolled to a stop by a tree, both feeling rather hopeless as the goblins shot off into the distance.

"Shall we take off our skates and run?" Rachel suggested. "We'd be quicker then."

"We still wouldn't be as quick as the goblins," Kirsty replied. "They're just flying along." She sighed. "If only we had fairy wings and could really fly!" she added. "Then we'd be able to catch up with them."

Just then, the girls heard a peal of silvery laughter above their heads, and they spotted Zoe the Skating Fairy zipping out of the tree to hover in the air in front of them! The girls had already met Zoe, and all the other Sporty Fairies, when they'd first started their adventure.

They were delighted to see her again.
Zoe had long red hair, and wore
a funky cropped top and skating shorts.
A pretty blue pendant hung around
her neck, sparkling in the sunshine.

"Did someone say they'd like some
fairy wings?" she asked, smiling and
twirling her wand between her fingers.
"I can help with that."

"Oh, thank you," Rachel said
eagerly. "We've spotted four goblins on
skates, Zoe, and we're sure they've got
your Magic Lace because they're
skating brilliantly!"

"Unlike everyone else here today,"
Kirsty added, as a girl on rollerskates
veered off the path nearby, just missing
a large bush.

Zoe winced as the girl fell over onto

the grass. Luckily, she was wearing a helmet and wasn't hurt. "Oops!" Zoe said. "I see what you mean, girls. Come behind this tree, out of sight, and I'll turn you into fairies."

Kirsty and Rachel did as she asked, and Zoe waved her wand over them. Immediately, a shower of sparkling fairy dust surrounded the girls and transformed them into fairies.

Rachel fluttered her wings in delight. "Come on!" she cried. "Let's catch up with those goblins."

"Fly high," Zoe reminded the girls. "We don't want anyone in the park to spot us."

The three fairies zoomed through the air until they caught sight of the four goblins down below.

"They're lining themselves up," Kirsty noticed. "What are they doing?"

Rachel stared. The goblins had split up, so that each one was the same distance away from the next. "Is it some kind of trap?" she wondered nervously. The friends watched as the goblin at the back of the line began skating along the path towards his friend. "He's got my Magic Lace!" Zoe exclaimed, pointing at a shimmering object in his hand. "What's he doing with it?"

As the goblin reached his friend, he handed the lace over. Then the second goblin skated off, while the first goblin stopped and watched him go.

"They're practising for a relay race," Kirsty realised.

"And using the Magic Lace as a baton!" Rachel added.

Up ahead, the fairies could see that
a third goblin was
waiting in position,
near a copse of
oak trees. Seeing
the oak trees gave
Rachel an idea.

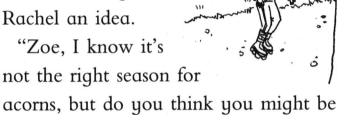

"Zoe, I know it's
not the right season for
acorns, but do you think you might be
able to magic some into those trees?"

"Yes, no problem," Zoe replied,
"but why?"

"If we can get to the trees before the
third goblin starts his part of the race,"
Rachel explained, "we can shower him
with magic acorns, and then, while
he's distracted, swoop down and grab
the lace!"

"That's a great idea!" Kirsty cried. "We'd better hurry, though; the second goblin will reach the third soon."

The three fairies sped along as fast as they could. Zoe pointed her wand at the trees, and Rachel and Kirsty smiled as they saw hundreds of sparkling fairy acorns appear amidst the leaves.

Meanwhile, down below, the second
goblin had handed the lace on.
The third goblin promptly set off on
his skates, through the trees, clutching
the Magic Lace. As he did so,
Zoe waved her wand again and
the branches began to shake.
Soon, lots and lots of glittering
green acorns were showering down
around the third goblin.

Kirsty's Sweet Idea

"Help!" yelled the goblin, covering his head with his hands. "What's happening?"

"There's the lace!" Zoe hissed, spotting it between his fingers. "If I use my magic to keep the branches still, will you two try to get it?"

"Of course," Kirsty replied eagerly.

Zoe touched her wand to the branch
in front of her, and all the trees stopped
showering acorns and became still. Kirsty
and Rachel immediately swooped down
towards the goblin's hand.

Unfortunately, now that the acorns
had stopped falling, the goblin had
uncovered his head and was staring up
at the tree. He soon caught sight of
Kirsty and Rachel speeding towards him.

"Where did you come from?" he
cried, trying to skate away from them.

But there were
so many acorns
littering the ground
that the wheels of
one skate jammed
and the goblin lost
his balance. His
arms flailed and
the sparkling lace
fell from his grip and
dropped to the ground.

Rachel's eyes lit up as she saw it fall,
and she plunged towards it. Her fingers
were just about to fold around the
Magic Lace when the goblin's
big bottom thundered to the ground,
trapping the lace underneath it.

Rachel and Kirsty only just managed
to dart out of the way in time to
avoid being squashed. They looked
despairingly at the fallen-down goblin,
and then at each other. There was no
way they could get the Magic Lace
now that the goblin was sitting on it.

The goblin picked himself up and
grabbed hold of the lace once more.
Then he stuck his tongue out at the

fairies. "Keep your sparkly acorns to yourself!" he snapped. "You're not getting the Magic Lace, and that's that!" Then, picking his way carefully through the acorns, he skated off towards the fourth goblin, further down the path.

Zoe put her hands on her hips. "Oh, we so nearly had it!" she sighed. "Well, we'll just have to make a new plan."

Rachel and Kirsty nodded and,
together, the three friends flew after
the goblin. They caught up to see
that the relay had now finished,
and the four goblins were shouting
at each other. The friends perched
on a branch to listen.

"If you can't go faster than that,
you'll be dropped from the team!"
the first goblin scolded the third.

"If you skate like that in the Fairyland Olympics, we'll lose," the second goblin added. "Jack Frost will be furious!"

"It wasn't my fault," the third goblin argued. "I was attacked!"

"Attacked?" scoffed the fourth goblin. "By what?"

"By...an army!" the third goblin declared. "An army of fairies. They bombarded me with magic acorns!"

"Tiny little acorns?" the first goblin sneered. "So what?"

"No, no," the third goblin protested. "Not tiny little acorns. Great enormous acorns. Acorns the size of footballs!"

Kirsty and Rachel tried not to laugh out loud as the goblin's story got wilder and wilder.

"They came at me from all angles," he went on dramatically. "I could have been squashed at any moment!"

The other goblins were wide-eyed. "Ooh, squashed!" the second one repeated, glancing around nervously.

The third goblin nodded. "I was lucky to escape with my life," he boasted. "I had to fight heroically to save the Magic Lace."

"Good work," the first goblin said, clapping him on the back. "How did you keep it safe?"

The third goblin hesitated. "Um..." he began.

Rachel, Kirsty and Zoe smiled at each other. He didn't want to admit that he'd kept the lace safe by sitting on it!

"I…I just managed to keep it out of their way," he replied at last.

Just then, a voice shouted from across the park, "Doughnuts! Come and get your lovely doughnuts! Free samples! Try before you buy!"

The girls looked round to see a man setting up a doughnut stall nearby. The goblins saw it too.

"Oooh, doughnuts," the fourth goblin said, licking his lips. "I'm hungry!"

The first goblin shook his head. "We don't have time for doughnuts," he said sternly. "We need to keep practising. And we're meant to be eating healthy food before the Olympics, not cakes!" He ignored the fourth goblin's dismayed look and began issuing orders. "So, we'll do the same practice run again, ending at this tree, OK?" He pointed to a stout oak by the side of the path. "As before, once you've completed your part of the race, come back here for a time-check. Now, everyone get in position!"

With a last longing look at
the doughnut stall, the fourth goblin
trudged back to his position. So did
the others.

Kirsty looked thoughtfully at
the hungry goblin. *Just how much does
he want a doughnut?* she wondered.
Enough to fall for a trick?

Trick or Treat?

"I've got an idea," Kirsty whispered
to her friends. "Zoe, do you think that
you could make me look like a goblin?"

Zoe looked at Kirsty thoughtfully.
"I think so," she replied. "I'd just have
to turn your clothes into a tracksuit,
make you the right height and tint
your skin green." She wrinkled her nose.

"If the goblins look closely at you, they'll be able to see you're not a real goblin, though."

"If my plan works, that won't matter," Kirsty replied.

"What *is* your plan?" Rachel asked curiously.

"Well, we need to get that hungry goblin to leave his spot on the race track. Then I'll take his place," Kirsty explained, "and when the third goblin skates up and hands over the Magic Lace, I'll skate away with it!"

"Brilliant!" Zoe cried. "And the lace's powers will mean you can whizz off super-fast!" she added.

"But how will we persuade the goblin to leave the track?" Rachel asked.

The doughnut man began shouting
again and Kirsty grinned.

"If you have a doughnut, Rachel, and
tempt the goblin with it, he might go to
the doughnut seller and get one for
himself," she said. "And then Zoe can
make me look like a goblin and I'll stand
in his place, ready to get the lace."

Zoe beamed. "One doughnut
coming up!" she cried, waving her
wand. With a fizz
of fairy dust, Rachel
grew to her usual
size, and a warm,
sugary doughnut
appeared in mid-air.
It hovered there for
a moment, then drifted
into Rachel's hand.

"Ooh, pleased to eat you," Rachel said, with a giggle. The doughnut did smell delicious. Then she winked at her friends. "Here I go!"

Rachel carefully climbed down the tree, and strode towards the goblin, waving the doughnut so that its yummy scent drifted under his nose. Then she took a bite. "Mmm-mmm!" she said loudly.

The goblin stared at her and licked his lips.

"This is soooo delicious," Rachel went on, taking another nibble.

The goblin glared. "Go away!" he snapped. "I'm trying to concentrate on the relay and you're putting me off."

"Sorry," Rachel said innocently. "It's just that this doughnut is scrumptious."

The goblin watched her take another bite, then a sly look crossed his face. Suddenly, he flung out an arm to try to grab the doughnut. Rachel darted out of the way.

"Give me that!" the goblin ordered greedily.

"Get one for yourself," Rachel replied.

"The man over there is giving out free samples."

The goblin glanced over his shoulder longingly, but then his face fell. "It's my turn to race soon," he said. "I'd better not."

"Oh, you've got plenty of time," Rachel told him. "Better not wait too long, though. The doughnut man may not have very many left..."

The goblin looked panicked at the thought of missing out on a sweet treat altogether, and with a last look at Rachel's delicious doughnut, he skated off at once.

Rachel looked up at Kirsty and Zoe as they flew down to the ground.

"It's goblin time for you!" Zoe said to Kirsty, and waved her wand.

Kirsty Races Into Trouble

Sparkly red fairy dust streamed
around Kirsty. She tingled all over,
then felt herself getting bigger and
bigger. Soon she was about half
her human size, and she looked
down to see that she was now
wearing a tracksuit and her hands
had turned green.

"Wow!" Rachel said. "You really do look a bit like a goblin."

"Not as sneaky as a real one, though," Zoe reassured her.

"I'll go and wait in the fourth goblin's position on the track," Kirsty said.

"OK," Zoe replied. "We'll meet you by the oak tree that marks the finishing line. Good luck!"

Kirsty stepped onto the path and checked over her shoulder to see where the third goblin in the relay was. He was skating right towards her, so she whipped her head back again. She didn't want him to get a proper look at her face. Her heart pounded with excitement. She hoped her plan was going to work.

She could hear the third goblin's skates now as he drew nearer, so Kirsty slowly began skating herself, her hand stretched out behind her ready to take the lace.

Then, just as she felt the third goblin
putting the Magic Lace into her palm,
she heard an indignant voice cry, "Hey!
It's my turn!"

Kirsty turned and saw that the fourth
goblin had returned, munching his
doughnut and looking astonished to see her
in his place. Kirsty could think of only one
thing to do: she grabbed the lace from
the third goblin and took off at top speed
before either of the goblins could reach her.

"What's going on?" she heard
the fourth goblin yell as she sped away.

Meanwhile, Zoe had transformed
Rachel back into a fairy and they had
zoomed to the finishing line, watching
everything from above. They saw
the third and fourth goblins stare at
each other, and then at Kirsty, who
was now whizzing away. Then they
saw it dawn on the goblins that Kirsty
wasn't actually a goblin at all.

"We've been tricked!" the goblin with
the doughnut shouted
furiously. "It was all
your fault, giving
her the Magic
Lace like that!
Couldn't you see it wasn't me?"

"It wasn't my fault!" the third goblin
retorted. "If you'd stayed in position,
like you were supposed to do, none
of this would have happened!"

"Well, we need to catch her,"
the goblin with the doughnut said.
"Right now!"

The two goblins began skating after
Kirsty. Now that they no longer had
the Magic Lace, they couldn't go
as quickly as before, but they kept on
skating, puffing and panting as they went.

Then Rachel noticed that the two
goblins who had skated the first part
of the relay had doubled back on
themselves. They were now making
their way towards the finishing line,
too, but from the opposite direction.
Suddenly, she saw one of them nudge
the other and point ahead at Kirsty,
who was zooming towards them.

"Oh, no!" Rachel cried. "The other two goblins have spotted Kirsty!"

Rachel and Zoe immediately set off towards Kirsty, too. The two goblins who had been first in the relay seemed to have guessed something was wrong, because they suddenly started skating much faster.

"They're going to try to head Kirsty off!" Zoe realised.

"Poor Kirsty," Rachel cried in horror. "She'll be caught in the middle of all four goblins!"

Rachel and Zoe flew towards Kirsty as fast as they could.

"I'll turn Kirsty into a fairy," Zoe
decided. "Then she can fly up into
the air, away from the goblins."

"What about the lace?" Rachel
reminded her. "It might be too heavy
for her to carry when she's a fairy."

Zoe shook her
head. "Don't
worry," she said.
"The Magic
Sporty Objects
change their size
according to who's
holding them. When Kirsty becomes
a fairy, the lace will magically become
its Fairyland size." Then she frowned
anxiously and flapped her wings harder.
"But we need to get to Kirsty before
the goblins do…"

Rachel nodded. They had to get to Kirsty in time, otherwise her friend would be at the mercy of four goblins!

Flying High

Down on the track, Kirsty glanced
over her shoulder to see that
the two goblins were still behind
her, glaring as they gave chase.
But when she looked ahead again,
she gasped in shock. Skating
straight towards her were the
first and second goblins.

Kirsty looked all around, but there was no way out. She couldn't skate off the path and onto the grass, because there was a fenced-off tennis court on one side of her and flowerbeds on the other. She was trapped!

The goblins were closing in and Kirsty felt sick with fright. They were so close now that she could hear them shouting at her to give back the lace.

Their arms were outstretched, reaching for the Magic Sporty Object.

"Help!" Kirsty cried, wondering where Zoe and Rachel were, and hoping they would hear her. "Help!"

And then, at the very last second, just as one of the goblins was about to seize the Magic Lace, she saw a cloud of bright sparkles swirl around her, and felt herself shrinking down and down and down...

Oh, what a relief it was to feel wings
on her back and find
that she was a fairy
once more! Kirsty
zipped up into
the air, flapping
her wings as hard
as she could, as
the goblins below
jumped up and down,
trying to grab her.

"Kirsty, are you OK?" Rachel cried, as
she and Zoe flew over, panting.

"Yes," Kirsty replied faintly. "That was
close, though. Thanks, Zoe!"

The three fairies landed on a branch
of a nearby oak tree to get their breath
back. Instantly, the goblins tried to climb
the tree. They still had their skates on,

though, so they were finding it
a struggle.

Zoe put her hands on her hips and
shouted down to them. "Any more
trouble from you lot and I really will
make magic acorns the size of footballs
to drop on you!" she warned. "And
then you'll be goblin pancakes!"

The goblins hesitated. "I don't want to be a goblin pancake!" wailed one, dropping down from the tree trunk.

"Nor me," chorused the others, stumbling away from the oak. Soon, the four of them were skating away as fast as they could.

Kirsty handed Zoe the Magic Lace, smiling.

Zoe looked delighted to have it back. "Thank you so much!" she breathed. She touched her wand to the lace and a flash of bright red sparkles surrounded it. "There," she said happily. "Now all will be well again with skaters everywhere."

The three of them flew down to the ground, and Zoe waved her wand over Kirsty and Rachel, magically turning them back to their normal size.

69

"Thanks again, girls," she said.
"Enjoy the rest of your time in the
park. You'll find skating much more
fun now, I promise."

"Thanks, Zoe," Rachel replied. "It
was great helping you. Goodbye!"

"Goodbye," Kirsty added.

"Bye, girls," Zoe said, and, with
a burst of red fairy dust that sparkled
for a second in the air, she was gone.

Rachel nudged Kirsty as a group of boys went by on in-line skates, whooping as they carried out some tricky-looking turns. "Look, everyone's skating well again," she said.

Rachel was right. Nobody was falling over any more. All the skaters and skateboarders looked as if they were enjoying themselves as they whizzed along.

Kirsty grinned. "I bet we'll be able to skate better now, too," she said happily. "Come on, let's find out. I'll race you to that tree!"

And the two friends skated off together, laughing as they went.

Another Magic Sporty Object was safely back with its fairy keeper – now there were just four left to find!

The Sporty Fairies

Rachel and Kirsty must now help

Naomi the Netball Fairy

Naomi has had her Magic Netball
stolen by the pesky goblins! Can Rachel
and Kirsty help her to get it back
so that netball can be fun again
for everyone?

Spring into Sport

"What shall we do after lunch, Kirsty?" asked Rachel Walker, as she finished her apple.

Kirsty Tate, Rachel's best friend, grinned. "You know what I'd really like to do?" she replied. "I'd like to find Naomi the Netball Fairy's Magic Netball!"

Rachel and Kirsty shared a very special secret. While holidaying on Rainspell Island, the two girls had become friends with the fairies, and now Rachel and Kirsty always helped out whenever there was a problem in Fairyland.

"Remember what Queen Titania told

us," Rachel reminded Kirsty. "We have to let the magic come to us."

"I know, but I'm feeling really impatient today," Kirsty replied. "If we don't find all the Magic Sporty Objects before I go home in a few days' time, Jack Frost and his goblins will win the Fairyland Olympics Cup!"

The Fairyland Olympics were due to take place at the end of the week, but mean Jack Frost had stolen the Sporty Fairies' seven Magic Sporty Objects. These magical objects made sure that sport was fun and exciting, as well as played fairly, in both the human world and Fairyland. But Jack Frost wanted his goblin servants to cheat their way to victory in the Fairyland Olympics, using the magic of the Sporty Objects to win

every single event. He had sent the
goblins into the human world to keep
the magic objects hidden away and
to practise their sports. But Rachel
and Kirsty had promised the Sporty
Fairies that they would try to get the
seven objects back before the fairy
games began.

Rachel sighed. "The missing objects
mean that sports in our world are
affected too," she added. "I wonder how
many netball games are going wrong
right now because Naomi's Magic
Netball is missing..."

Read the rest of

Naomi the Netball Fairy

to find out what magic happens next...

Calling all parents, carers and teachers!
The Rainbow Magic fairies are here to help
your child enter the magical world of reading.
Whatever reading stage they are at, there's
a Rainbow Magic book for everyone!
Here is Lydia the Reading Fairy's guide to
supporting your child's journey at all levels.

The Rainbow Magic Reading Challenge

Well done, fairy friend – you have completed the book!
This book was worth 5 points.

See how far you have climbed on the **Reading Rainbow**
on the Rainbow Magic website below.

The more books you read, the more points you will get,
and the closer you will be to becoming a Fairy Princess!

How to get your Reading Rainbow
1. Cut out the coin below
2. Go to the Rainbow Magic website
3. Download and print out your poster
4. Add your coin and climb up the Reading Rainbow!

There's all this and lots more at
www.rainbowmagicbooks.co.uk

You'll find activities, competitions, stories, a special
newsletter and complete profiles of all the
Rainbow Magic fairies. Find a fairy with your name!

The Sporty Fairies

Special thanks to
Narinder Dhami

ORCHARD BOOKS

First published in Great Britain in 2008 by
The Watts Publishing Group
This edition published in 2015 by
The Watts Publishing Group

1 3 5 7 9 10 8 6 4 2

© 2008 Rainbow Magic Limited.
© 2008 HIT Entertainment Limited.
Illustrations copyright Orchard Books 2008

HiT entertainment

A CIP catalogue record for this book is available from the British Library.

ISBN 978 1 40835 324 0

Printed in Great Britain by Clays Ltd, St Ives plc

MIX
Paper from
responsible sources
FSC® C104740
FSC
www.fsc.org

The paper and board used in this book are made from wood from responsible sources

Orchard Books
An imprint of Hachette Children's Group
Part of The Watts Publishing Group Limited
Carmelite House, 50 Victoria Embankment, London EC4Y 0DZ

An Hachette UK Company
www.hachette.co.uk
www.hachettechildrens.co.uk

Naomi
the Netball
Fairy

by Daisy Meadows

Join the Rainbow Magic Reading Challenge!

Read the story and collect your fairy points to climb the
Reading Rainbow at the back of the book.

This book is worth 5 points.

The Fairyland Palace

Fairyla...

Car Park

Coaches

Cooke Football Stadium

Riding Stables

Netball Courts

Football Pitches

Tippington Town

LEISURE CENTRE

Swimming Pool

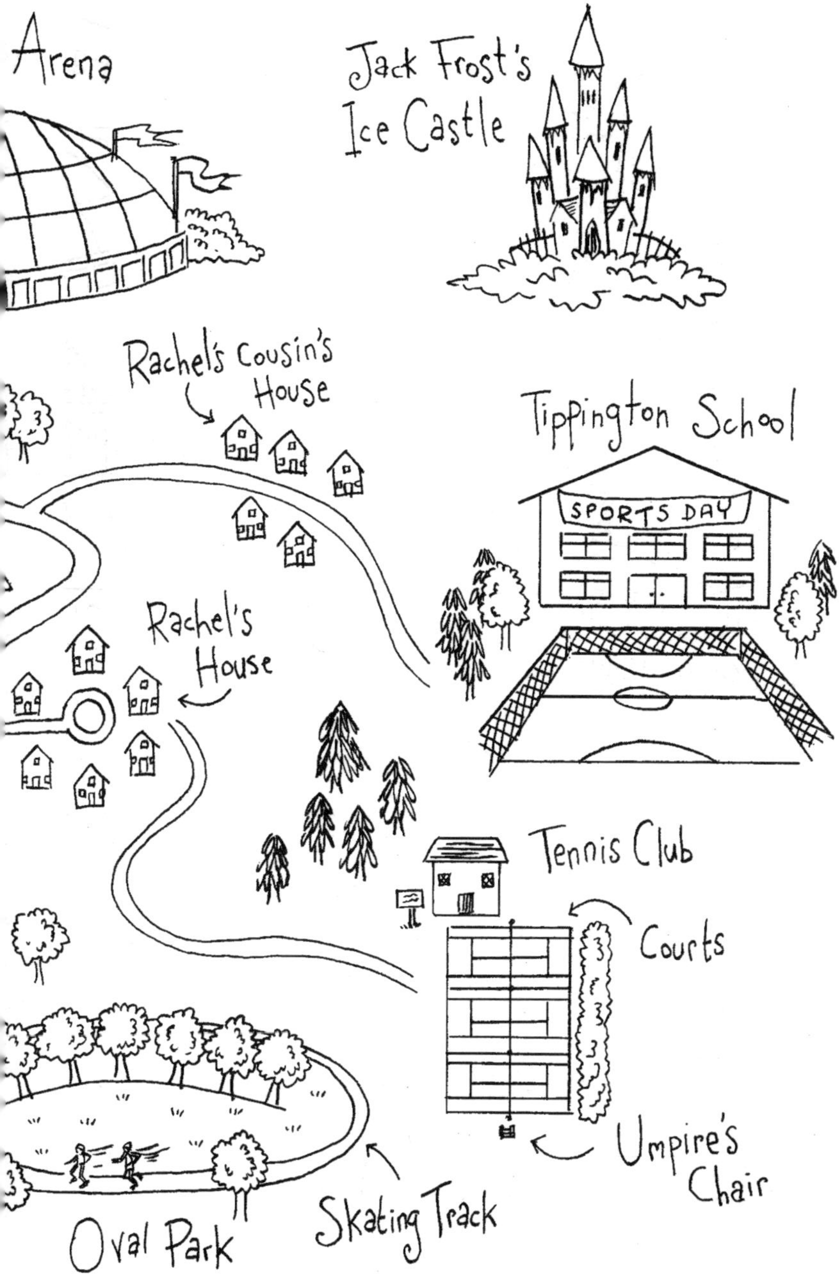

Arena

Jack Frost's
Ice Castle

Rachel's Cousin's
House

Tippington School

SPORTS DAY

Rachel's
House

Tennis Club

Courts

Umpire's
Chair

Oval Park

Skating Track

The Fairyland Olympics are about to start,
And my expert goblins are going to take part.
We will win this year, for I've got a cunning plan.
I'm sending my goblins to the arena in Fairyland.

The Magic Sporty Objects that make sports safe and fun,
Will be stolen by my goblins, to keep until we've won.
Sporty Fairies, prepare to lose and to watch us win.
Goblins, follow my commands, and let the games begin!

Contents

Spring into Sport

"What shall we do after lunch, Kirsty?" asked Rachel Walker, as she finished her apple.

Kirsty Tate, Rachel's best friend, grinned. "You know what I'd really like to do?" she replied. "I'd like to find Naomi the Netball Fairy's Magic Netball!"

9

Rachel and Kirsty shared a very special secret. While holidaying on Rainspell Island, the two girls had become friends with the fairies, and now Rachel and Kirsty always helped out whenever there was a problem in Fairyland.

"Remember what Queen Titania told us," Rachel reminded Kirsty. "We have to let the magic come to us."

"I know, but I'm feeling really impatient today," Kirsty replied. "If we don't find all the Magic Sporty Objects before I go home in a few days' time, Jack Frost and his goblins will win the Fairyland Olympics Cup!"

The Fairyland Olympics were due
to take place at the end of the week,
but mean Jack Frost had stolen the
Sporty Fairies' seven Magic Sporty
Objects. These magical objects made
sure that sport was fun and exciting,
as well as played fairly, in both the
human world and Fairyland. But Jack
Frost wanted his goblin servants to
cheat their way to victory in the
Fairyland Olympics, using the magic
of the Sporty Objects to win every single
event. He had sent the goblins into the
human world to keep the magic objects
hidden away and to practise their sports.
But Rachel and Kirsty had promised
the Sporty Fairies that they would try
to get the seven objects back before
the fairy games began.

Rachel sighed. "The missing objects mean that sports in our world are affected too," she added. "I wonder how many netball games are going wrong right now because Naomi's Magic Netball is missing!"

"Well, we've already found Helena's Hard Hat, Francesca's Football and Zoe's Lace," Kirsty pointed out.

Rachel nodded. "We can't let Jack Frost and his goblins win the cup by cheating," she said solemnly. "Especially as King Oberon told us that the cup is filled with good luck. Imagine all the mischief the goblins could cause with lots of luck to help them!"

Just then, Rachel's mum came into the kitchen. "Girls, have you finished your lunch?" Mrs Walker asked. "I don't know if you've decided what you want to do this afternoon, but I thought this might be fun." And she put a leaflet down on the table.

"'Spring into Sport!'" Rachel read aloud. "'On Tuesday, from 9.30 am, come and try a new sport at Tippington Leisure Centre – absolutely free!'"

Kirsty flipped the leaflet open. "Look!" she exclaimed. "Rounders, badminton, athletics, cricket and netball…" Kirsty glanced meaningfully at Rachel.

The Sporty Fairies had told the girls
that any goblin who had one of the
Magic Sporty Objects would be
attracted to that sport, especially as
the goblins wanted to practise their
skills for the Fairyland Olympics. So
Rachel and Kirsty knew it was possible
that the goblin with the Magic Netball
might turn up at the leisure centre.

"Why don't you go and try out
a few sports?" Rachel's mum suggested,
clearing away the plates.

"Good idea, Mum," said Rachel,
jumping up from the table.

"It does sound like fun," Kirsty
agreed.

The girls pulled on their trainers
and headed into the village. The leisure
centre was just behind the High Street.

There were football and cricket pitches in front of the building, and matches were taking place on all of them. There were also groups of people standing around, waiting to have a go.

"Looks like we're not the only ones who want to 'Spring into Sport!'" Kirsty said as they headed towards the glass doors. "Do you think the goblins might be here?"

Rachel nodded. "Maybe, but if they are, it's going to be difficult to spot them with so many people around."

The girls went inside the leisure centre and watched a badminton match. Then they peeked into the studio where a keep-fit class was taking place.

"Let's go and check out the netball courts," Rachel suggested, as they passed the gym. "They're outside, near the athletics track."

When the girls arrived, they found that matches were in progress on all the netball courts except for one. Two teams were limbering up next to the empty court, ready to start a game.

"Everything looks normal," Kirsty said quietly. "I can't see any goblins."

"Neither can I," Rachel agreed. Then she noticed a girl hurrying towards them. "Kirsty, that's my friend Abby, from school!" Rachel exclaimed. She waved at the girl as she rushed past. "Hey, Abby!"

Abby stopped, looking rather flustered. "Oh, hi, Rachel," she said. "Sorry, I was in such a rush, I didn't notice you there.

Is this your friend Kirsty?"

Rachel nodded.

"Hello, Abby," said Kirsty. "Is there something wrong? You look a bit worried."

"Oh, everything's going wrong today!" Abby replied, heaving a huge sigh. "I'm in a netball team with my friends, and we've just been challenged to a game by some boys who call themselves 'The Mean Green Netball Team'."

"The Mean Green Netball Team?" Rachel repeated. "What a name!"

"Yes, and they are mean!" Abby told her. "They've beaten all the other teams easily. They've even painted their hands with green paint and they're wearing green masks." She shook her head. "Talk about taking the team name

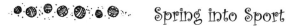

too seriously!"

Kirsty felt a shiver of excitement run down her spine. She glanced at Rachel and could see that her friend was thinking exactly the same thing: could The Mean Green Netball Team be a group of goblins?

Rachel and Kirsty Join the Team

Abby bit her lip nervously. "The trouble is," she went on, "two of our players haven't turned up. The game is starting in a few minutes, and we haven't even got a full team! I was just on my way into the leisure centre to see if I could find some people to make up the numbers."

21

Rachel glanced at Kirsty again.
We simply have to find out if the
green players are goblins, Rachel
thought. And this is our chance!

"Kirsty and I could play for your
team," Rachel offered. "Couldn't we,
Kirsty?"

Kirsty nodded as Abby's face lit up.

"Oh, would you?" Abby said,
gratefully. "That would really help
us out!"

"We're not wearing the right clothes, though," Kirsty said, glancing at the tracksuit bottoms she and Rachel had on.

"Don't worry about that," Abby told her, ushering the girls towards the court. "It's a taster session, not a proper match. Some of the players are wearing netball skirts and others are wearing tracksuits."

"OK," said Kirsty. "I'd better warn you, though, I'm not that great at netball."

Abby smiled. "Actually, nobody's playing very well today except The Mean Green Netball Team," she confessed. "Everyone seems to have butter fingers and two left feet, including me."

Rachel looked sympathetic. She and Kirsty both knew why everyone was being clumsy. It was because Naomi's Magic Netball was missing.

"We'll just have to do our best," Rachel declared in a determined voice, and Kirsty nodded.

"Well, I've seen you playing netball at school, Rachel, and I know you're good at shooting," Abby replied as they reached the court, "so you can be our secret weapon!"

Rachel blushed. "I'll try and get a couple of goals," she promised.

Abby found two bibs at the side of the court and handed them to Rachel and Kirsty.

"Kirsty, you're in defence and Rachel, you're in attack," she explained as they ran onto the court. "Come and meet the rest of the team."

Abby took Rachel and Kirsty over to a small group of girls who were standing at one end of the court. They all looked rather nervous.

"Cheer up, everyone!" Abby exclaimed. "I've found two more players for us."

The rest of the team brightened up
immediately.

"That's great!" said a tall girl with
fair hair. "We're going to need a full
team. The Mean Green Netball Team
is really good!"

Rachel and Kirsty looked over at
The Mean Green Netball Team,
which was practising its ball skills at
the other end of the court. The team

members wore baseball caps and were passing the ball swiftly and confidently to each other.

"They're definitely goblins, Kirsty," Rachel whispered, catching a glimpse of a pointy green nose under one of the caps.

"I know," Kirsty agreed quietly. "And look at that goblin spinning the netball on his finger over there."

Rachel stared at the goblin and gasped as she saw that the ball spinning on his finger was surrounded by a faint  shimmer of purple sparkles. "It's Naomi's Magic Netball!" she exclaimed in a low voice. "Yes! Now all we have to do is get it back," Kirsty pointed out.

"Let's get started," called the umpire, blowing her whistle. "We're playing for just fifteen minutes today." She flipped a coin in the air and turned to the biggest goblin, who was captain.

"Heads!" called the captain.

The umpire examined the coin.

"Heads it is," she announced.
"The Mean Green Netball Team
will start the game."

The goblins dashed quickly into their
positions. The umpire blew her whistle
and immediately the
goblin in the centre
flung the Magic
Netball to the
goblin on his
right. Kirsty and
another defender
moved to block
him, but the second
goblin threw the ball high
over their heads and straight towards
one of the goblin shooters. The next
moment, the ball was whizzing cleanly
through the hoop.

"One-nil," called the umpire as the goblins whooped with glee and gave each other high-fives.

Kirsty glanced down the court at Rachel in dismay. The goblins were ahead, and none of their team had even touched the ball yet!

The game restarted, but once again the goblins were quickly in control.

30

After a succession of brilliant passes, the goblin shooter sidestepped Kirsty and popped the ball through the hoop again.

"Two-nil!" the umpire shouted.

Rachel watched helplessly from the other end of the court as the goblins moved the ball around swiftly and smoothly and scored lots of goals. None of Abby's team could even get near the ball because the goblins were too quick for them, and Rachel realised that this meant the human players weren't benefiting from the magic of Naomi's netball. She looked across the court at Kirsty and shook her head sadly.

They were never going to get hold
of the Magic Netball at this rate.

Then one of the goblins tried to
lob the ball high up into the air
towards one of his
team-mates, but
Abby jumped up
and actually
managed to
intercept the ball.

"Abby!" Rachel
shouted eagerly,
waving her arms.
"Over here!"

Abby flung the ball
straight towards Rachel, but just
as Rachel was about to catch it,
a goblin leapt in front of her and
batted the ball away.

"Oh, no!" Rachel sighed. She stood beneath the goal, watching sadly as the goblins swept the ball speedily down to the other end of the court. As she stood there, a shower of purple sparkles suddenly rained down around her. Rachel glanced up in surprise to see Naomi the Netball Fairy sitting on the rim of the hoop!

Fairy Help at Hand

Naomi waved at Rachel and fluttered down to join her. She wore a blue and purple netball skirt and shirt, and matching trainers. Her blonde hair was neatly tied up with ribbons and a purple headband.

"Don't be sad, Rachel," Naomi whispered, landing lightly on Rachel's shoulder. "I'm sure we'll find another way to get my netball back."

"I hope so," Rachel said eagerly.
"It's great to see you, Naomi!"

Naomi grinned and slipped quickly into
the pocket of Rachel's tracksuit bottoms.

At that moment, the umpire blew her
whistle. "The Mean Green Netball Team
win eleven-nil!" she announced.

The goblins cheered loudly.
Meanwhile, Abby's team trudged away.

"What a whitewash!"
Abby groaned, as she
and Kirsty came
over to Rachel.
"We hardly
touched the ball
from start to finish.
But thanks for taking
part, you two.

We're going to try out some of the other sports now, would you like to come?"

"Thanks, but we thought we'd look around a bit more first," Rachel said. "We'll come and find you later."

As Abby waved goodbye, Rachel drew Kirsty to the side of the court, away from the celebrating goblins.

"Look who's here," Rachel whispered.

"Hello, Kirsty," called Naomi, fluttering out of Rachel's pocket.

"Oh, Naomi!" Kirsty exclaimed. "Thank goodness you're here. We really need your help to get the Magic Netball."

Naomi pointed her wand at the gleeful goblins. "We'd better stay close to them and wait for our chance to grab the ball," she suggested. "Look, they're leaving."

Two other teams had turned up to play
a match, and the goblins were hurrying
off the court, still chattering excitedly.
Their captain led the way, carrying
the Magic Netball.

Naomi ducked back into Rachel's
pocket, and the girls followed the goblins,
being careful to keep a little way behind
so that they wouldn't be spotted.

"Right, we're going to practise shooting now," the captain said bossily, leading his team into the leisure centre. "We'll use one of the indoor courts where it's nice and quiet."

The other goblins groaned.

"That's boring!" one complained loudly. "Can't we do something else? We're great at shooting already!"

The captain glared at him. "What do you mean *boring*?" he snapped. "There's always room for improvement. Now, come on!"

He marched onto one of the indoor courts and the other goblins trailed after him, grumbling to each other.

Kirsty, Rachel and Naomi peeked through the open doors as the goblins began shooting at one of the hoops with the Magic Netball.

"They're scoring almost every time," Rachel whispered.

The goblins were now so confident that they began doing silly tricks. They tried turning their backs to the hoop and shooting over their shoulders or from between their legs. Sometimes they missed, but most of the time they still managed to score goal after goal.

Naomi sniffed as the ball whizzed through the hoop yet again. "It's my Magic Netball that's doing all the work," she said crossly. "Those goblins wouldn't be any good without it."

"Oh!" Kirsty gasped. "Naomi, you've given me an idea. I think I know how we can get your Magic Netball back!"

Magic in the Air

"What do we have to do, Kirsty?" Rachel asked.

"Naomi, can you magic up a new netball?" Kirsty asked. "One that sparkles as if it's magic?"

Naomi nodded. "Sure," she replied. "But it won't really have magical powers. It'll just be an ordinary netball."

43

"That's fine," Kirsty replied. "But can you also use your magic to make the goblins' hoop repel any netball that's thrown at it?"

This time Naomi frowned. "I can do that with a simple wave of my wand," she said slowly, "but the spell won't last for long because my Magic Netball is so powerful. Eventually it will overcome any repelling magic I put on the hoop."

"Well, my plan shouldn't take too long to put into action," said Kirsty. "We just need to convince the goblins that the real Magic Netball isn't working properly, and that we have a new, improved netball that's full of magic! Then they might do a swap."

Rachel looked puzzled. "But the goblins will only want our ball if they see us scoring lots of goals with it," she pointed out.

"Exactly," Kirsty agreed.

"But, how is that going to work?" Rachel asked, looking even more confused. "Naomi just said that the other netball won't really be magic at all. And the goblins will only believe it's magical if it lands in the hoop every time!"

Kirsty grinned at her. "That's where you come in, Rachel," she explained. "You'll have to use your brilliant shooting skills to persuade the goblins that we really do have a magic netball!"

Rachel gulped. "You mean I have to shoot and get the ball through the hoop every time?"

"That's the plan," Kirsty replied. "Do you think you can do it, Rachel?"

"I don't know." Rachel looked a little anxious. "I might not be very good at shooting today because the Magic Netball isn't in its proper place."

"But it is in the same room," Naomi said. "So some of its magic will help you."

"OK," Rachel agreed. "I'll just concentrate and try to score a goal each time the goblins are looking. It's difficult but it's not impossible."

"Go, Rachel!" Naomi said, twirling around with excitement. "And here's your new netball." She raised her wand and made a circle of pink sparkles in mid-air.

Then the sparkles transformed
themselves into a netball which
glittered slightly, just like the magic
one. The ball floated towards Rachel,
and she caught it neatly.

The goblins were taking turns to
shoot at the hoop, but they had
begun arguing about who was next.

"It's my go!" the smallest goblin
screeched, trying to grab the ball
from the captain.

"I'm in charge," the captain growled crossly. "I'll decide who's next!"

"I think it's time someone else had a turn at being captain," another goblin declared.

"No way!" the captain yelled.

As the goblins argued furiously, Naomi grinned at Rachel and Kirsty. "Now's my chance to put the repelling spell on the hoop while the goblins aren't looking," she whispered.

Naomi pointed her wand at the goblins' hoop and a rush of purple sparkles streamed through the air. Rachel and Kirsty watched as the sparkles surrounded the hoop and then quickly began to fade.

But, just then, a tall, thin goblin happened to glance up. "Hey!" he shouted, staring at the faint gleam around the hoop. "What's that? It looks like fairy magic."

Rachel, Kirsty and Naomi stared at each other in dismay. Had their plan failed already?

Girls Go into Action

The goblins all stared up at the hoop,
but the last few sparkles had already
vanished.

"What are you talking about?"
the captain snapped. "There's nothing
there!"

"You're seeing things!" another goblin
teased, and they all burst out laughing.

"But I did see some sparkles," the tall goblin insisted. He rushed forward and peered carefully up at the hoop, while the other goblins waited impatiently.

"OK, I can't see any fairies," the tall goblin mumbled sheepishly.

"Your shot," the captain ordered, thrusting the ball into the goblin's arms.

The goblin squinted at the hoop and then threw the Magic Netball towards it. The ball curved upwards in a perfect arc, but, as it fell downwards, it missed the hoop completely.

"What's happening?" the tall goblin squawked, looking confused as the ball fell to the ground.

"You're useless, that's what's happening!" another goblin said scornfully. He grabbed the netball and launched a shot himself. But again, although the ball whizzed straight towards the hoop, it missed at the last minute.

"The goblins are starting to look worried," Naomi whispered to the girls as the captain also tried a shot and failed. "I think it's time for you to do your bit, Rachel."

Rachel, Kirsty and Naomi came out from their hiding place behind the doors to the netball court. They hurried to the hoop at the free end of the court, the new netball tucked under Rachel's arm.

The goblins didn't notice them because they were arguing about why the Magic Netball didn't seem to be working properly.

"Here goes," Rachel murmured, positioning herself in front of the hoop and carefully taking a shot. The ball rose smoothly and fell cleanly through the hoop.

"Well done, Rachel!" Naomi and Kirsty cried, applauding loudly.

Feeling more confident, Rachel tried again. This time the ball caught the edge of the hoop slightly, but it still went in.

As Kirsty and Naomi cheered, Kirsty glanced over her shoulder. The goblins were staring at them from the other end of the court.

"The goblins aren't happy," Kirsty whispered.

Rachel grinned and immediately scored another perfect goal.

This was too much for the goblins

and they all came rushing over, one of them carrying Naomi's Magic Netball.

"How come you're scoring lots of goals and we're not?" the captain demanded.

"Oh, it's because I have this wonderful Magic Netball," Rachel replied, holding the ball up.

"But we have the Magic Netball!" one
of the goblins said, looking puzzled.

Naomi peered at their netball. "Oh,
you've got the old Magic Netball," she
told the goblins dismissively. "This is the
brand-new, super Magic Netball!"

Rachel took another shot. The goblins all
muttered enviously to each other as once
again the ball zoomed through the hoop.

"This new Magic Netball is better than the old one!" the captain declared.

"Yes, give us the new netball!" the goblins clamoured eagerly. One of them even began creeping towards Rachel.

Naomi frowned. "If you try to steal the Magic Netball, I'll turn Rachel and Kirsty into fairies and we'll all fly away," she told the sneaky goblin, lifting her wand. "Then you'll never get the new netball!"

The goblins looked at each other in dismay.

"Well, can we just have a go with the new Magic Netball?" the small goblin begged. "Please?"

Naomi looked thoughtful for a moment. "Well," the fairy said reluctantly, "we'll swap our new netball for your old one if you agree to leave here and go back to Goblin Grotto immediately."

"Done!" the goblin with the ball agreed eagerly, holding it out towards Rachel. But just as Rachel was about to take it...

"STOP!" the captain yelled in a very suspicious voice.

The goblin snatched the ball away from Rachel's grasp, and she glanced anxiously at Kirsty and Naomi. Had the captain guessed what was going on? "Why do you want us to go back to Goblin Grotto?" the captain demanded. "Because if you stay in the human world much longer, someone's going to realise you're goblins!" Naomi replied quickly.

"Your tracksuits and baseball caps aren't a very good disguise. And you know we can't allow humans to find out about Fairyland and Goblin Grotto."

The captain nodded thoughtfully. "That's true," he muttered. "OK, make the switch!"

The goblin held out Naomi's netball again, but, this time, before Rachel could take it, the captain sprang forward.

"STOP!" he shouted.
"Oh, make your
mind up,"
the goblin
grumbled,
whisking the ball
away from
Rachel once more.

"We agree to the
swap on one condition," the captain
declared. He pointed at Kirsty. "She
hasn't had a go at scoring. I want to
make sure the new Magic Netball works
on everyone, so let's see her score a goal!"

"Me?" Kirsty gulped. She'd never scored
a netball goal in her life!

"You can do it, Kirsty," Rachel
whispered encouragingly, handing her
the ball.

Naomi fluttered over to Kirsty. "Take a deep breath and steady yourself," she told her quietly. "Focus on the hoop and make your shot as smooth as possible. And, most important of all, take your time."

Kirsty nodded, feeling very nervous. Her palms were sweating as she held the netball up and fixed her eyes on the hoop, trying to remember exactly how Rachel had scored all her wonderful goals.

After a moment, Kirsty made her shot. The ball flew through the air, and Rachel, Naomi and Kirsty all gasped as it touched the hoop and rattled around the rim. Would the ball fall inside or out?

A Glorious Goal

It seemed to take for ever, but,
finally, the ball dropped through
the hoop. Kirsty almost burst with
relief as she grinned delightedly
at Rachel and Naomi.

"OK, we definitely want that
netball," the captain decided
quickly.

Kirsty picked up the ball and

swapped with the goblin who had Naomi's Magic Netball. "Now, remember, you're going straight home to Goblin Grotto," Naomi reminded them.

"Yeah! We can show the new Magic Netball to Jack Frost," the goblin with the ball cried. "He's going to be very pleased with us!"

"Give the ball to me," the captain ordered.

"No!" the goblin retorted rudely, running off across the court. The other goblins chased after him, and Rachel, Kirsty and Naomi laughed.

"They're going to be disappointed when they find out that the new Magic Netball isn't actually magical at all," said Rachel.

"Oh, but it is!" Naomi replied with a wink. "We didn't lie. The new ball is magical because it's made of fairy magic. It just doesn't make people good at netball, that's all!" She grinned, flew over to Kirsty and took the Magic Netball. As Naomi touched it, the ball shrank to its Fairyland size.

Then Naomi touched the ball with her wand, making it glitter even more brightly for a moment.

"Thank you, girls," she cried. "Netball games everywhere will go well again, now, and I must return to Fairyland and tell the other Sporty Fairies the good news."

She smiled at Rachel and Kirsty as she spun the Magic Netball around quickly on one finger. "Keep up the good work." And Naomi zoomed out of the door, leaving a trail of dazzling purple sparkles behind her.

"Well, you were right, Rachel," Kirsty said happily as they went in search of Abby and her friends. "The magic did come to us!"

"And now we're going to have fun trying out other sports," Rachel laughed. "And hopefully we'll have more exciting adventures with the Sporty Fairies, too!"

The Sporty Fairies

Rachel and Kirsty must now help

Samantha the Swimming Fairy

Jack Frost's naughty goblins have stolen Samantha's Magic Goggles, so nobody can swim properly! Can Rachel and Kirsty help Samantha to outwit the goblins and get the goggles back?

Swimming Pool Puzzle

"Fetch, Buttons!" Rachel Walker called, throwing her dog's favourite ball down the garden.

Kirsty Tate, Rachel's best friend, who was staying with the Walkers for a week of the Easter holidays, smiled. "Buttons loves exercise, doesn't he?" she said, as Buttons bounded after the ball. "We're nearly as fit as him, after the sporty week we've had so far!"

Rachel grinned. Unknown to her parents, she and Kirsty had been on a new fairy adventure this week, helping the Sporty Fairies track down their

missing Magic Sporty Objects. Rachel felt
as if she and Kirsty were the luckiest girls
in the world, being friends with the fairies.

"Good dog!" said Rachel's dad, coming
out into the garden with Mrs Walker, as
Buttons rushed back with the ball in his
mouth. Buttons dropped the ball at
Rachel's feet, then went to his water
bowl to drink thirstily.

"Phew, it's hot," Mrs Walker said,
fanning herself. "The perfect day for a
swim, I'd say."

Rachel and Kirsty looked at one
another excitedly. Swimming would be
a great idea – especially as Samantha the
Swimming Fairy's Magic Goggles were
still missing.

"Ooh, yes, can we go swimming?"
Rachel asked.

"Tippington Pool is closed," Mr Walker pointed out, "so you'd have to go to Aqua World in the next village." Then he frowned. "But the car's being serviced in the garage; I won't be able to drive you there."

"You could get the bus," Mrs Walker said. "The 41 goes all the way there. If you take your mobile, Rachel, you can let me know when you'll be back."

"Yay!" cheered Rachel and Kirsty together. They both dashed inside to pack their swimming things, then Rachel's mum walked them to the bus stop...

Read the rest of

Samantha the Swimming Fairy

to find out what magic happens next...

RAINBOW magic

Calling all parents, carers and teachers!
The Rainbow Magic fairies are here to help
your child enter the magical world of reading.
Whatever reading stage they are at, there's
a Rainbow Magic book for everyone!
Here is Lydia the Reading Fairy's guide to
supporting your child's journey at all levels.

Starting Out

Our Rainbow Magic Beginner Readers are perfect for first-time readers who are just beginning to develop reading skills and confidence. Approved by teachers, they contain a full range of educational levelling, as well as lively full-colour illustrations.

1

Developing Readers

Rainbow Magic Early Readers contain longer stories and wider vocabulary for building stamina and growing confidence. These are adaptations of our most popular Rainbow Magic stories, specially developed for younger readers in conjunction with an Early Years reading consultant, with full-colour illustrations.

2

Going Solo

The Rainbow Magic chapter books - a mixture of series and one-off specials - contain accessible writing to encourage your child to venture into reading independently. These highly collectible and much-loved magical stories inspire a love of reading to last a lifetime.

3

www.rainbowmagicbooks.co.uk

"Rainbow Magic got my daughter reading chapter books. Great sparkly covers, cute fairies and traditional stories full of magic that she found impossible to put down" - Mother of Edie (6 years)

"Florence LOVES the Rainbow Magic books. She really enjoys reading now" - Mother of Florence (6 years)

The Rainbow Magic Reading Challenge

Well done, fairy friend – you have completed the book!
This book was worth 5 points.

See how far you have climbed on the **Reading Rainbow**
on the Rainbow Magic website below.

The more books you read, the more points you will get,
and the closer you will be to becoming a Fairy Princess!

How to get your Reading Rainbow
1. Cut out the coin below
2. Go to the Rainbow Magic website
3. Download and print out your poster
4. Add your coin and climb up the Reading Rainbow!

There's all this and lots more at
www.rainbowmagicbooks.co.uk

You'll find activities, competitions, stories, a special
newsletter and complete profiles of all the
Rainbow Magic fairies. Find a fairy with your name!

The Sporty Fairies

For all the children of
Newbridge Primary School

Special thanks to
Sue Mongredien

ORCHARD BOOKS

First published in Great Britain in 2008 by Orchard Books
This edition published in 2017 by The Watts Publishing Group

1 3 5 7 9 10 8 6 4 2

Copyright © 2008 Rainbow Magic Limited.
Copyright © 2008 HIT Entertainment Limited.
Illustrations copyright © Orchard Books, 2008

HIT entertainment

A CIP catalogue record for this book is available from the British Library.

ISBN 978 1 40835 325 7

Printed in Great Britain by Clays Ltd, St Ives plc

Orchard Books
An imprint of Hachette Children's Group
Part of The Watts Publishing Group Limited
Carmelite House, 50 Victoria Embankment, London EC4Y 0DZ

An Hachette UK Company
www.hachette.co.uk
www.hachettechildrens.co.uk

Samantha
the Swimming
Fairy

by Daisy Meadows

Join the **Rainbow Magic Reading Challenge!**

Read the story and collect your fairy points to climb the
Reading Rainbow at the back of the book.

This book is worth 5 points.

The
Fairyland
Palace

Fairyl·

Car Park

Coaches

Riding Stables

Cooke Football
Stadium

Netball Courts

Football
Pitches

Tippington
Town

LEISURE CENTRE

Swimming Pool

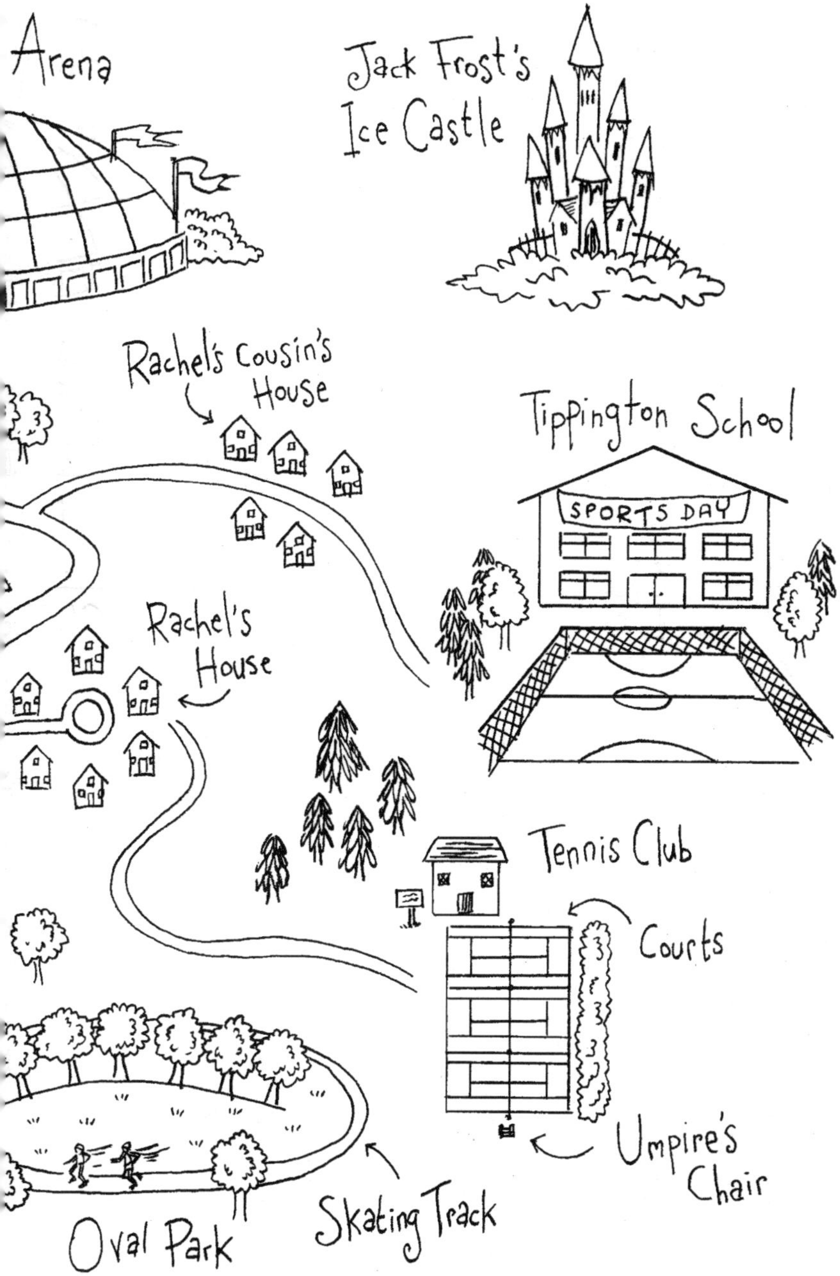

Arena

Jack Frost's
Ice Castle

Rachel's Cousin's House

Tippington School

SPORTS DAY

Rachel's House

Tennis Club

Courts

Umpire's Chair

Oval Park

Skating Track

The Fairyland Olympics are about to start,

And my crafty goblins are going to take part.

We'll win this year, for I've got a cunning plan.

I'm sending my goblins to the arena in Fairyland.

The Magic Sporty Objects that make sports safe and fun,

Will be stolen by my goblins, to keep until we've won.

Sporty Fairies, prepare to lose and to watch us win.

Goblins, follow my commands, and let the games begin!

Contents

Swimming Pool Puzzle

"Fetch, Buttons!" Rachel Walker called, throwing her dog's favourite ball down the garden.

Kirsty Tate, Rachel's best friend, who was staying with the Walkers for a week of the Easter holidays, smiled. "Buttons loves exercise, doesn't he?" she said, as the dog bounded after the ball.

9

"And we're nearly as fit as him, after the sporty week we've had so far!"

Rachel grinned. Unknown to her parents, she and Kirsty had been on a new fairy adventure this week, helping the Sporty Fairies track down their missing Magic Sporty Objects. Rachel felt as if she and Kirsty were the luckiest girls in the world, being friends with the fairies.

"Good dog!" said Rachel's dad,
coming out into the garden with Mrs
Walker, as Buttons rushed back with the
ball in his mouth. Buttons dropped the
ball at Rachel's feet, then went to his
water bowl to drink thirstily.

"Phew, it's hot," Mrs
Walker said, fanning
herself. "The perfect
day for a swim,
I'd say."

Rachel and Kirsty
looked at one another
excitedly. Swimming would
be a great idea – especially as
Samantha the Swimming Fairy's
Magic Goggles were still missing.

"Ooh, yes, can we go swimming?"
Rachel asked.

"Tippington Pool is closed," Mr
Walker pointed out, "so you'd have to
go to Aqua World in the next village."
Then he frowned. "But the car's being
serviced in the garage; I won't be able
to drive you there."

Kirsty felt disappointed, as she loved
swimming. At the start of the week, she
and Rachel had discovered that naughty
Jack Frost had sent his goblins to steal
the Sporty Fairies' Magic Sporty Objects.
When the objects were with the Sporty
Fairies – or in their lockers in the
Fairyland Arena – they made sure that
sports in the human world and in
Fairyland were safe, fun and played
fairly. But, when they weren't in place,
sports everywhere were ruined and
disrupted and only those people very

close to a Magic Sporty Object were good at that particular sport.

The Fairyland Olympics were due to be held soon and Jack Frost wanted his goblins to use the objects' powers to cheat in the contest and win the big prize – a golden cup full of luck. Kirsty and Rachel knew that the goblins were practising hard for their events, so the goblins with Samantha's Magic Goggles were sure to be found in a swimming pool somewhere.

"You could get the bus," Mrs Walker said. "The 41 goes all the way there. If you take your mobile, Rachel, you can let me know when you'll be back."

"Yay!" cheered Rachel and Kirsty together. They both dashed inside to pack their swimming things, then Rachel's mum walked them to the bus stop.

They didn't have to wait long before
a bus pulled up. The girls waved goodbye
to Mrs Walker and sat
together at the back
of the bus where
the seats were
slightly higher
and they had
a good view out
of the window.

Kirsty gazed out at the houses and
the bus set off.

As they waited at some traffic
lights, Kirsty noticed that they had
stopped near Tippington Swimming Pool.
A sign outside read 'CLOSED FOR
MAINTENANCE'. The building had
a glass front, tinted at the bottom to

prevent people looking in, but clear
at the top.

A huge pipe wrapped around the outside
of the building. Kirsty guessed it must be
a water slide.

Suddenly, Kirsty noticed a flash of
green pop up above the level of the
tinted glass. She blinked and stared.
What was that?

The green thing appeared again and
Kirsty let out a gasp. She was sure she'd
just seen a goblin!

Goblins Galore!

Kirsty nudged Rachel. "Look!" she hissed, pointing.

As the girls watched, the goblin popped up again and Rachel's eyes shone excitedly. "How lucky that you spotted him!" she exclaimed. "If he's in there, I bet Samantha's Magic Goggles are, too."

"But why does he keep popping up and

17

then vanishing?" Kirsty wondered, as the goblin appeared above the tinted glass once more.

"He must be bouncing on the diving board," Rachel giggled. She stood up and pressed the bell to tell the driver that they wanted to get off. "Come on," she said, "let's investigate. We can go to Aqua World afterwards."

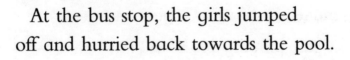

Kirsty jumped up eagerly. Another fairy adventure was beginning!

At the bus stop, the girls jumped off and hurried back towards the pool.

"I didn't notice the goblin wearing any goggles," Kirsty said.

"Nor me," Rachel agreed. "But maybe there are two of them in there."

Kirsty and Rachel went round to the side of the building and pressed their faces up against the glass so that they could see in more clearly. Then they both gasped in amazement.

"There are goblins everywhere!" Rachel cried.

The whole pool was full of green goblins of all sizes. Some were diving, others were swimming laps and some were just playing in the shallow end.

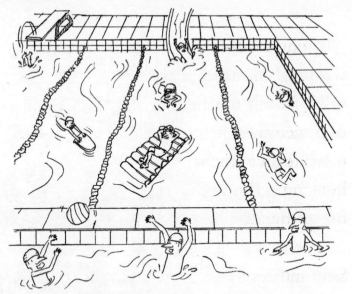

"We'd better get in there, and start looking for the Magic Goggles," Kirsty said. "It might take us a while."

The girls crept along, looking for a way inside the building. Unfortunately, the whole place seemed securely locked up. Then Rachel heard footsteps and the girls darted behind a bush. They peeped through the leaves, and saw a figure coming towards them.

It was a goblin, wrapped in a big, stripy beach towel, and wearing a white swimming hat and red goggles on his head!

"Are those Samantha's Magic Goggles?" Rachel asked Kirsty in a whisper.

Kirsty shook her head. "I think those are just ordinary ones," she whispered back. "They don't look magical. The other Magic Sporty Objects have all sparkled with fairy magic."

The girls watched as the goblin walked to a nearby tree, and climbed up into its branches. Then he started crawling along a thick branch that led all the way to an open window in the building. The goblin reached the window and wriggled through it, disappearing from view.

"So that's how they've been getting in," Kirsty said. "Let's try it."

She and Rachel climbed up the tree, along the branch and in through the window, just as the goblin had done. They found themselves in a tiled corridor.

"I know where we are," Rachel said confidently. "The pools are this way."

She led Kirsty down the corridor. Faint shouts and squeals of excitement echoed up from the pools, and the girls crept along cautiously, not wanting to be seen.

At the end, they peeped around the corner. Kirsty saw two pools, a large one with a water slide at the back, and a smaller, shallower pool in front. In the small pool, seven goblins, all wearing nose clips, floated on the surface. They lay with their heads together in the middle of the pool, while their legs pointed out to the sides. It reminded Kirsty of a wheel, with goblins for spokes.

"What are they doing?" she murmured.

Rachel tried not to laugh out loud. "They're practising synchronised swimming!" she hissed. "I can't see any sparkly shimmers on their goggles though, can you?"

The girls peered carefully at all the goggles on the goblins' heads, but they all seemed quite ordinary.

Then the goblins flipped over into handstands, with their bodies underwater and their legs sticking out, toes pointed. They each lowered their left legs, and turned in the water at the same time.

"Come on, let's get past them while they're underwater," Kirsty said. "Then we can search the main pool."

The girls raced past the small pool, and hid behind a pile of lilos. Then Rachel noticed something interesting ahead. She nudged Kirsty. "Do you see those floats over there?" she asked, pointing to a stack of them at the water's edge. "They're shimmering with pale pink sparkles!"

"Maybe the Magic Goggles have been left there," Kirsty whispered. "Let's go and check."

The two friends ran over for a closer look. There was no sign of the Magic Goggles, but both girls smiled when they saw what was causing the sparkles. Perched on the top of the pile of floats, her tiny legs dangling over the edge, was Samantha the Swimming Fairy!

Goggles Under Guard

Samantha had long dark hair, and
a pink and black swimming costume,
with a pretty pink sarong-style skirt.
"Hello there, girls!" she said cheerfully.

"Hello," Rachel smiled. "We're on
the hunt for your Magic Goggles!"

"Me too," Samantha said. "I can
sense that they're in this building."

She grinned at the girls. "But I can't
let you stay in those jeans and T-shirts!
Let's get you something more suitable
to wear…" She waved her wand and
a stream of glittering, powder-pink
fairy dust swirled from its tip, tumbling
around the girls. Seconds later, their
clothes were replaced with two-piece
swim-skirt suits. Rachel's was lilac
with a silvery dolphin pattern on it,
and Kirsty's was turquoise with
a gold seashell print.

"That's more like it!" smiled
Samantha.

"Ooh, thank you," Kirsty said,
admiring her costume. "Now we should
try looking in the big pool for your
goggles, Samantha. None of the goblins
in the little pool have them."

Rachel pointed to the spectators' seats
that ran along the side of the main
pool. "Let's nip behind those," she
suggested. "Then we can peep out to
look for the goggles but stay hidden."

"Good idea," Samantha agreed.

Together, the two girls and their fairy
friend crept behind the plastic seating,
and peered out between the chairs.

Kirsty noticed a goblin wearing
a T-shirt that said LIFEGUARD on the

front. He was sitting up in a high chair
by the side of the pool and shouting
instructions to the other goblins.
But Kirsty's eye was caught by what
dangled from his left hand — a pair
of sparkling pink goggles! "Over there,"
she whispered excitedly to her friends.
"I think it's the Magic Goggles!"

Samantha beamed. "Yes, it is!"
she cheered quietly. "Well spotted!"

"Now we just need to think of
a way to get hold of them," Rachel
said thoughtfully.

"Why don't I turn you two into
fairies?" Samantha suggested. "That
way we can try to fly really close to the
lifeguard without him noticing – and,
with a bit of luck, sneak the goggles
straight out of his hand."

Rachel and Kirsty nodded.

"Yes, let's try it," Kirsty said eagerly.

Samantha waved her wand, and,
once more, a cloud of light pink
sparkles spun around the girls. This
time they felt themselves shrinking
down and down until they were
fairy-sized.

It's always so exciting, turning into a fairy! thought Kirsty. She fluttered her wings happily, loving the way they shone with all the colours of the rainbow under the bright lights above the pool.

"Let's go goggle-grabbing," Rachel giggled as she zoomed into the air. Kirsty and Samantha followed, keeping as close to the ceiling as they could so that the goblins in the pool wouldn't notice them.

As they got closer to the lifeguard, Rachel could hear him bragging.

"I'm the lifeguard, that means I'm in charge," he was telling some other goblins. "And I say no splashing, no cannon-balling and no dunking!"

"We're only having a bit of fun," a small goblin replied. "You're a meanie!"

"Rules are rules!" retorted the lifeguard. He pointed to his T-shirt in a self-important manner. "Read the T-shirt!" he ordered. "I'm the lifeguard – what I say goes!"

Kirsty, Rachel and Samantha hovered behind the lifeguard's chair, waiting for a good moment to grab the goggles. But the lifeguard kept a tight hold of them, swinging them from his finger and thumb.

Now a different goblin with a cheeky expression approached. "It's my turn to have those," he said, pointing to the Magic Goggles. "You've had them for ages, and you're not even using them! I want to wear them on the water slide."

"Certainly not," the lifeguard sniffed. "Water-sliding is not an Olympic sport! We've come here to practise Olympic water events, remember, not to mess about on slides."

"But—" the other goblin began.

But the lifeguard was in full flow now. "Have you forgotten that the Fairyland Olympics is only two days away?" he continued. "Two days! That's all you've got! So practise your lengths instead of sliding, please. Jack Frost won't be very happy if he hears about this."

The other goblin stomped off in
a huff, and Kirsty thought the lifeguard
goblin looked rather smug as he
watched him go. He
twirled the Magic
Goggles around
one of his
knobbly fingers.

The three fairies
exchanged glances
and flew a little nearer, hoping to
slip the goggles off the lifeguard's
finger and zoom away with them.
But, just then, there came a cry
of alarm from the water.

"Help!"

Kirsty, Rachel and Samantha all
turned to see what was happening.
A goblin was flailing around in the

deep end at the opposite side of the pool, thrashing his arms and splashing water everywhere. "Help!" he spluttered again, and then slipped below the surface.

A Cheeky Thief

The lifeguard immediately put the
Magic Goggles on and dived into
the water with a huge splash.

The three fairies watched as he
powered across the pool, his long green
arms scooping the water in a perfect
front crawl. In just a few strong strokes,
he'd reached the struggling goblin and

was towing him to safety. He popped
the Magic Goggles on top of his head
as he reached the side of the pool.

"Wow!" Rachel said admiringly.
"What a brilliant swimmer – or, rather,
your goggles are brilliant, Samantha,
for making him swim so well."

Samantha nodded. "They are very
powerful goggles," she agreed proudly.
Then her eyes widened. "What's
happening over there?"

Kirsty and Rachel looked and saw
that the goblin who'd asked to borrow
the Magic Goggles was now swimming
up behind the lifeguard goblin.
Suddenly, he stretched
out his arm and
swiped the Magic
Goggles from the
top of the
lifeguard's head.
Then he swam off
with them towards
the water slide.

"He is *so* cheeky!"
Rachel exclaimed.

"The lifeguard didn't notice a thing,"
Kirsty added, watching as the lifeguard
pulled the struggling goblin out of the
water and onto the poolside.

The rescued goblin spluttered and coughed. "I thought I was going blind!" he wailed dramatically.

"Blind? Why?" the lifeguard asked.

The rescued goblin coughed again. "I got water in my eyes and it stung," he explained.

"Ahh," the lifeguard said, wagging a finger. "If you want to keep water out of your eyes, you need a pair of goggles like mine."

The rescued goblin frowned. "But you're not wearing any goggles," he replied, sounding confused.

The lifeguard clicked his tongue in an impatient sort of way. "Well, I keep them up here when I'm not actually swimming," he explained, pointing a finger at the top of his head, where the Magic Goggles had been just seconds earlier.

"Up where? I can't see them!" the rescued goblin said, completely bewildered now.

The lifeguard rolled his eyes. "Then you need glasses, not goggles!" he snapped. "Or maybe a new brain," he muttered. "Honestly!"

Samantha, Kirsty and Rachel couldn't help laughing.

"Come on, that rescued goblin's fine. Let's find the cheeky goblin who took my goggles," Samantha said.

The three friends flew across the pool, looking out for the tell-tale shimmer of the Magic Goggles. The water was still full of goblins, but after a minute or so, Kirsty caught a glimpse of pink sparkles and pointed them out to her friends.

"There!" she said. "He's swimming in the deep end, do you see?"

Rachel and Samantha both watched.
The goblin with the goggles was
slicing through the water with a very
impressive front crawl, wearing
the goggles as he swam.

The three friends zoomed after the
goblin but he was going very fast.
Before they'd had a chance to catch
up, he'd reached the other end of the
pool and the entrance to the water
slide. He got out, pushing the goggles

onto his head. Then he rushed up
the steps to the slide, barging through
a whole crowd of other goblins who were
waiting their turn. "Let me past! Get out
of the way!" he shouted. "Goblin with
goggles coming through!"

It wasn't long before a scuffle broke out
among the goblins at the top of the slide.
"Stop pushing!" shouted one.
"Wait your turn!" cried another.

"You're treading on my toes!" yelped somebody else.

Kirsty, Rachel and Samantha looked at one another despairingly. How were they going to get the goggles back now that they were so tightly surrounded by goblins?

Spotted!

Rachel racked her brains, but it was hard to concentrate because a noisy argument was taking place between two goblins in the pool down below.

"It's my turn for the rubber ring," said the taller of the goblins, trying to snatch it from the other's hands.

"No way! I only just got it!" the

second goblin snapped. "It won't fit you anyway. It's too small for you."

The tall goblin looked offended and splashed the second goblin in the face before swimming away angrily.

But their squabble had given Rachel an idea. "Samantha, would you be able to magic up an inflatable ring?" she asked.

"Of course," said Samantha, holding out her wand.

"And could you make it slightly smaller than usual, please?" Rachel went on.

Samantha nodded. "No problem," she replied. "Why?"

"Well," Rachel began, "I was thinking that we could hold it at the end of the water slide. Then, when the goblin with the Magic Goggles comes shooting out of the slide, he'll go straight into the rubber ring, and if the rubber ring's a little tight, it might trap his arms by his sides."

Kirsty grinned. "And then we'll be able to take the Magic Goggles right off his head!" she finished. "Brilliant, Rachel!"

Samantha was smiling. "I love it," she agreed. "And I can use my fairy magic to make the ring just the right size to pin the goblin's arms to his sides without hurting him. Let's see…" She muttered some magical words and waved her wand. Bright pink fairy dust shot from the end of it, and then a tiny turquoise rubber ring appeared from nowhere, hovering in mid-air.

Rachel beamed. "Perfect," she said, flying to take hold of it.

"I made it tiny for now, so we can carry it easily and it won't be spotted by the goblins," Samantha said. "I'll magic it bigger when the time comes to use it. Let's take it over to the end of the slide and wait for our goblin."

The three of them carried the rubber ring through the air and hovered near the exit to the water slide. Lots of goblins were shooting down the slide, one after another, and splashing into the pool.

"There's our goblin," Kirsty said,
spotting him as he lay on his tummy at
the top of the slide. "But how are we
going to track where he is when he's
in the tube?" she asked. "It's going to
be tricky to catch the right goblin if we
don't know when our goggled-goblin's
going to pop out."

Samantha winked and waved her

wand. A stream
of sparkles shot
through the air
towards the goblin
as he pushed off
into the tube.
"There," she
giggled. "I've just
made his shorts
glow extra-brightly.

56

We should be able to see them shining
through the slide, even when he's in
the tube."

Rachel laughed. "There he is!" she
cried, pointing to a twisty section of
the slide where a bright blue glow
shone through the tube.

"He's getting nearer," Kirsty said,
as they saw the blue glow whizz round
the bendy bit of pipe and approach the
last section. "Let's get into position!"

Samantha waved her wand to make the rubber ring bigger. She and the girls were just preparing to lower it into the right spot, when they heard a cry go up from further down the pool.

"Hey, look out! Pesky fairies near the slide!"

Kirsty glanced over her shoulder and gulped. Several angry-looking goblins were pointing and swimming towards them.

She looked nervously at Rachel and Samantha. "We won't be able to catch the goblin on the slide if all the goblins come after us," she cried. "What are we going to do?"

Making Waves

"I'll take care of this," Samantha said, and pointed her wand at the water. A flurry of bubbles and sparkles streamed from the tip of her wand and into the pool. Immediately, huge waves appeared and began rolling towards the crowd of goblins as if a wave machine had been switched on.

At first, the goblins tried to
plough through the waves
and reach the fairies,
but then Samantha
magicked up a load
of bodyboards
and water toys.

"Hey, I'm
a super-surfer!"
one goblin shouted,
grabbing a board
and riding a
wave back to
the shallow end.
"Woohoo!"

All the goblins
wanted to be super-surfers
after that, some lying on
boards and coasting along on the

waves, while others tried to
jump up and stand. Soon
they were all whooping
with glee and playing
in the waves,
all thoughts of
the fairies
completely
forgotten.
Rachel and
Kirsty couldn't
help but chuckle.
"They won't
bother us any
more," Samantha
said. "Now let's get
the one with my goggles.
Look, he's just about to
come out of the chute!"

Sure enough, the goblin with the Magic Goggles was coming down the final run.

The three fairies gripped the rubber ring tightly.

"Here he comes!" Kirsty cried, and, a second later, the goblin with the Magic Goggles burst headfirst from the slide, straight into the rubber ring!

Thanks to Samantha's magic, the ring
was just the right size to pin his arms to
his sides, and when the girls let go, the
goblin was left
bobbing upright
in the water
like a big
green cork.

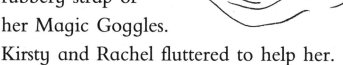

Samantha
flew over and
tugged at the
rubbery strap of
her Magic Goggles.
Kirsty and Rachel fluttered to help her.

"Hey!" shouted the goblin, scowling.
"Those goggles are mine!"

"Oh, no, they're not," Samantha told
him sternly. As the goggles came free,
they shrank to their Fairyland size and

Samantha dangled
them in front
of his face.
"Besides," she
went on with
a cheeky smile,
"I don't think
they would
fit you now!"

Samantha touched her wand to
the goggles and they sparkled even
more brightly for a moment. Kirsty
and Rachel knew that now the Magic
Goggles were back with Samantha,
their powers would start working
again, and swimming would be fun
and safe in the human world and
throughout Fairyland.

"Hurrah!" Rachel cheered happily,

as she, Samantha and Kirsty zoomed
safely up and out of the goblin's reach.
Then Samantha put on her Magic
Goggles and used her magic to calm
the waves and lift the ring off the
goblin, setting him free.
He splashed off
miserably to
join his friends.

The lifeguard,
seeing what had
happened, shouted
grumpily, "Everyone out of the pool.
It's time to go back to Jack Frost's
castle."

All the goblins clambered reluctantly
out of the pool, collected their towels
and clothes, and marched off. It was
very quiet once they'd gone.

"What a mess!" Kirsty said, gazing
down at all the floats, rings and
bodyboards still bobbing about in
the water.

"This won't take long to clear up,"
Samantha promised, and waved her
wand again. In a swirl of light pink
fairy dust, the floats and toys rose
up out of the water and put themselves
tidily away, the rubber rings rolling into
the cupboard like big colourful wheels.

Once the pool was back to normal, the three friends flew out through the open window, and Samantha used her magic to turn Kirsty and Rachel back into girls wearing outdoor clothes once more.

"I'd better go to Fairyland, to make sure everything's ready for the swimming events in the Fairyland Olympics," Samantha said, kissing Rachel and Kirsty goodbye. "Thank you so much for your help. Where are you going now?"

"We need to catch a bus to Aqua World," Rachel said.

Samantha nodded and waved her wand in a complicated pattern. A pink glittery ticket appeared in each girl's hand. "This'll be quicker," Samantha said.

"When you're ready, just touch the
tickets together. They're full of special
fairy dust, and will take you straight to
Aqua World."

"Oh, thank you!" Kirsty cried,
looking at her ticket in delight.
What an exciting day this was turning
out to be.

The girls said goodbye to Samantha
and watched as she flew off into the
distance.

"That was fun," Rachel said, holding her ticket out towards Kirsty's. "And I'm really looking forward to doing some swimming myself, now."

"Me too," Kirsty agreed, touching her ticket to Rachel's and feeling herself getting swept up by fairy magic. "But not as much as I'm looking forward to how we get there!"

**Now Kirsty and Rachel
must help...**

Alice the Tennis Fairy

Read on for a sneak peek...

"Isn't it a gorgeous day, Kirsty?"
said Rachel Walker happily. She
and her best friend, Kirsty Tate, were
walking along a country path not far
from the Walkers' house, enjoying the
sunshine. "And it would be even better
if we could find another Magic
Sporty Object!"

"Yes!" Kirsty agreed. "It's only two
more days until the Fairy Olympics, and
Alice the Tennis Fairy's Magic Racquet
and Gemma the Gymnastics Fairy's
Magic Hoop are still missing."

Rachel and Kirsty had promised to
help their friends, the Sporty Fairies,
find their seven Magic Sporty Objects.
Sports in both the human and the fairy
worlds were being disrupted because
these objects had been stolen by Jack
Frost and his goblin servants.
Jack Frost was determined that his goblin
team would win the Fairy Olympics and
the cup filled with good luck.

He knew that the power of the Magic
Sporty Objects meant that anyone close
to one of them immediately became
brilliant at that particular sport, so he
had sent his goblins into the human
world with each object, and told them to
practise for the fairy games.

As the girls walked on down the lane,
Rachel suddenly noticed a strange sign

pinned to a tree. "Look at that sign,"
she remarked, pointing it out
to Kirsty.

The words on the sign had been
painted very messily in bright green
paint. "'Goblindon'," Kirsty read aloud.
"And there's an arrow with the words
'Entrance to Tippington Tennis Club –
this way' written underneath it,"
she added.

"Oh, no!" Rachel exclaimed. "This
has got goblin mischief written all
over it! Mum and I have played tennis
at the club once or twice and there
are always lots of people around.
What if the goblins have been spotted
by someone?"

Kirsty looked worried. The girls knew
that nobody in the human world was

supposed to find out about Fairyland and its inhabitants.

"We must find out what's going on," Kirsty said urgently. "If the goblins are at the tennis club, they might have Alice's Magic Racquet…"

"Good thinking," Rachel agreed.

As the girls hurried off towards the tennis club entrance, they suddenly heard a loud voice coming from behind the hedge.

"Attention, goblins!" the voice announced. "I shall now explain the rules of the tournament."

"The goblins are having a tennis tournament!" Rachel exclaimed. "Instead of Wimbledon, it's Goblindon!"

"There's only one rule," the goblin went on. "I'm the umpire in charge of this tournament, so what I say, goes!"

He chuckled loudly, but Rachel and Kirsty could hear the sound of other goblins muttering and complaining.

"How many of them *are* there?" Kirsty asked with a frown...

Read Alice the Tennis Fairy to find out what adventures are in store for Kirsty and Rachel!

Meet the
Friendship Fairies

When Jack Frost steals the Friendship Fairies' magical objects, BFFs everywhere are in trouble! Can Rachel and Kirsty help save the magic of friendship?

www.rainbowmagicbooks.co.uk

Calling all parents, carers and teachers!
The Rainbow Magic fairies are here to help
your child enter the magical world of reading.
Whatever reading stage they are at, there's
a Rainbow Magic book for everyone!
Here is Lydia the Reading Fairy's guide to
supporting your child's journey at all levels.

Starting Out

1

Our Rainbow Magic Beginner Readers are perfect for first-time readers who are just beginning to develop reading skills and confidence. Approved by teachers, they contain a full range of educational levelling, as well as lively full-colour illustrations.

Developing Readers

2

Rainbow Magic Early Readers contain longer stories and wider vocabulary for building stamina and growing confidence. These are adaptations of our most popular Rainbow Magic stories, specially developed for younger readers in conjunction with an Early Years reading consultant, with full-colour illustrations.

Going Solo

3

The Rainbow Magic chapter books – a mixture of series and one-off specials – contain accessible writing to encourage your child to venture into reading independently. These highly collectible and much-loved magical stories inspire a love of reading to last a lifetime.

www.rainbowmagicbooks.co.uk

"Rainbow Magic got my daughter reading chapter books. Great sparkly covers, cute fairies and traditional stories full of magic that she found impossible to put down" - Mother of Edie (6 years)

"Florence LOVES the Rainbow Magic books. She really enjoys reading now" - Mother of Florence (6 years)

The Rainbow Magic
Reading Challenge

Well done, fairy friend – you have completed the book!
This book was worth 5 points.

See how far you have climbed on the **Reading Rainbow**
on the Rainbow Magic website below.

The more books you read, the more points you will get,
and the closer you will be to becoming a Fairy Princess!

How to get your Reading Rainbow
1. Cut out the coin below
2. Go to the Rainbow Magic website
3. Download and print out your poster
4. Add your coin and climb up the Reading Rainbow!

There's all this and lots more at
www.rainbowmagicbooks.co.uk

You'll find activities, competitions, stories, a special
newsletter and complete profiles of all the
Rainbow Magic fairies. Find a fairy with your name!

RAINBOW
magic ®

The Sporty Fairies

Special thanks to
Narinder Dhami

ORCHARD BOOKS

First published in Great Britain in 2008 by Orchard Books
This edition published in 2017 by The Watts Publishing Group

1 3 5 7 9 10 8 6 4 2

Copyright © 2008 Rainbow Magic Limited.
Copyright © 2008 HIT Entertainment Limited.
Illustrations copyright © Orchard Books, 2008

HiT entertainment

A CIP catalogue record for this book is available from the British Library.

ISBN 978 1 40835 326 4

Printed in Great Britain by Clays Ltd, St Ives plc

MIX
Paper from
responsible sources
FSC® C104740
www.fsc.org

The paper and board used in this book are made from wood from responsible sources

Orchard Books
An imprint of Hachette Children's Group
Part of The Watts Publishing Group Limited
Carmelite House, 50 Victoria Embankment, London EC4Y 0DZ

An Hachette UK Company
www.hachette.co.uk
www.hachettechildrens.co.uk

Alice
the Tennis
Fairy

by Daisy Meadows

Join the Rainbow Magic Reading Challenge!

Read the story and collect your fairy points to climb the
Reading Rainbow at the back of the book.

This book is worth 5 points.

The Fairyland Palace

Fairy

Car Park

Coaches

Cooke Football Stadium

Riding Stable

Netball Courts

Football Pitches

Tippington Town

LEISURE CENTRE

Swimming Pool

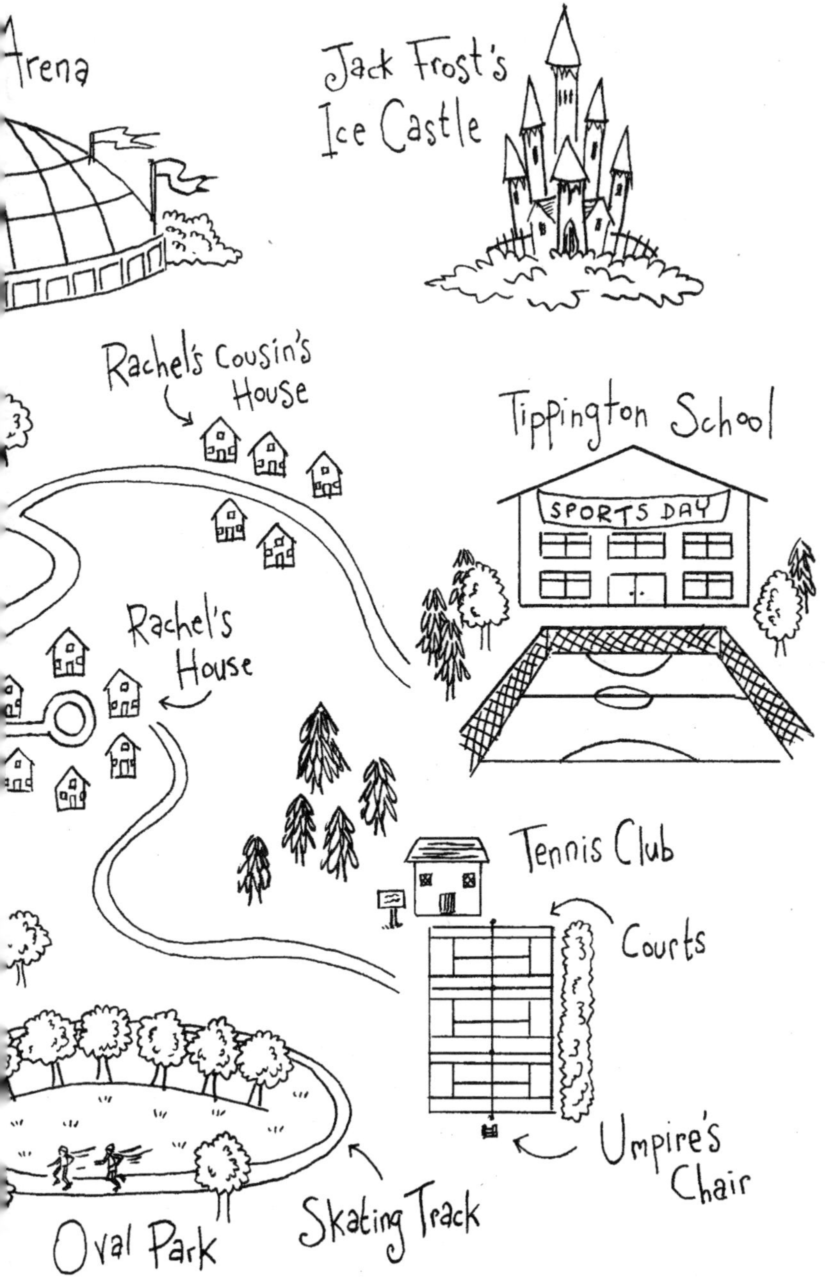

Arena

Jack Frost's
Ice Castle

Rachel's Cousin's
House

Tippington School

SPORTS DAY

Rachel's
House

Tennis Club

Courts

Umpire's
Chair

Oval Park

Skating Track

The Fairyland Olympics are about to start,

And my expert goblins are going to take part.

We will win this year, for I've got a cunning plan.

I'm sending my goblins to the arena in Fairyland.

The Magic Sporty Objects that make sports safe and fun,

Will be stolen by my goblins, to keep until we've won.

Sporty Fairies, prepare to lose and to watch us win.

Goblins, follow my commands, and let the games begin!

Contents

Goblindon

"Isn't it a gorgeous day, Kirsty?" said Rachel Walker happily. She and her best friend, Kirsty Tate, were walking along a country path not far from the Walkers' house, enjoying the sunshine. "And it would be even better if we could find another Magic Sporty Object!"

9

"Yes!" Kirsty agreed. "The Fairyland Olympics start tomorrow, and Alice the Tennis Fairy's Magic Racquet and Gemma the Gymnastics Fairy's Magic Hoop are still missing."

Rachel and Kirsty had promised to help their friends, the Sporty Fairies, find their seven Magic Sporty Objects. Sports in both the human and the fairy worlds were being disrupted because these objects had been stolen by Jack Frost and his goblin servants.

Jack Frost was determined that his goblin team would win the Fairyland Olympics and the cup filled with good luck.

He knew that the power of the Magic Sporty Objects meant that anyone close to one of them immediately became brilliant at that particular sport, so he had sent his goblins into the human world with each object, and told them to practise for the games.

As the girls walked on down the lane, Rachel suddenly noticed a strange sign pinned to a tree. "Look at that," she remarked, pointing it out to Kirsty.

Goblindon
Travel to
Vrington
tennis club
this way →

The words on the sign had been painted very messily in bright green paint. "*Goblindon*," Kirsty read aloud. "And there's an arrow with the words '*Entrance to Tippington Tennis Club – this way*' written underneath it," she added.

"Oh, no!" Rachel exclaimed. "This has got goblin mischief written all over it! Mum and I have played tennis at the club once or twice and there are always lots of people around. What if the goblins have been spotted by someone?"

Kirsty looked worried. The girls knew that nobody in the human world was supposed to find out about Fairyland and its inhabitants.

"We must find out what's going on," Kirsty said urgently. "If the goblins are at the tennis club, they might have Alice's Magic Racquet."

"Good thinking," Rachel agreed.

As the girls hurried off towards the tennis club entrance, they suddenly heard a loud voice coming from behind the hedge.

"Attention, goblins!" the voice

announced. "I shall now explain
the rules of the tournament."

"The goblins are having a tennis
tournament!" Rachel exclaimed.
"Instead of Wimbledon, it's *Goblindon!*"

"There's only one rule," the goblin
went on. "I'm the umpire in charge of
this tournament, so what I say, goes!"

He chuckled loudly, but Rachel and
Kirsty could hear the sound of other
goblins muttering and complaining.

"How many of them *are* there?"
Kirsty asked with a frown.

Rachel put a finger to
her lips. "We're right
near the tennis courts
here," she whispered.
"Let's look through
the hedge."

The girls pushed some leaves aside and peered through the hedge. Both of them tried not to gasp aloud at the scene in front of them. Tippington Tennis Club was full of goblins!

Tennis Time

Kirsty and Rachel glanced at each other in dismay. All the goblins were wearing tennis whites and they were limbering up as they prepared for the tournament.

"Luckily there don't seem to be any humans around," Rachel murmured.

"Look, Rachel!" Kirsty said suddenly.

17

"See the goblin up there on the umpire's chair?"

Rachel glanced across the court and saw a big goblin standing on the umpire's chair, looking very pleased with himself. In his hand he held a pink tennis racquet that shimmered in the sunlight.

"He's got Alice's Magic Racquet!" Rachel gasped.

"We *must* try to get it back," Kirsty whispered.

"As you all know, the Goblindon tournament has been designed to perfect your tennis skills," the goblin umpire went on, "so I want to see lots of brilliant shots and some really fancy footwork! The Fairyland Olympics are coming up, and we want to beat those pesky fairies and win the cup of good luck for Jack Frost!"

All the goblins cheered as the umpire waved the Magic Racquet in the air.

"The winner of Goblindon will receive a special prize," the umpire announced. "He will become Keeper of the Magic Racquet for the day!"

The goblins cheered again as they stared longingly at the Magic Racquet.

"They *all* want to win it!" Kirsty exclaimed.

"Yes, although I think the umpire would rather keep it himself," Rachel pointed out, as the goblin umpire lovingly stroked the racquet's pink handle. Then he nodded at two goblins standing on the sidelines.

"Bring on the ball machine!" he shouted.

The goblins began to push a massive ball machine onto one end of the court, right in front of the hedge where Kirsty and Rachel were standing. The girls jumped back quickly, afraid of being seen.

"Let's go to the club entrance," Rachel whispered. "We can watch from there, and maybe we'll get a chance to grab Alice's racquet."

The girls hurried along the lane towards the tennis club gates.

As they did so, they heard the umpire explaining that, in the first round of the tournament, the goblins would be competing against the ball machine.

"Any goblin who manages to return the ball, or dodge out of the way without being hit, for a total of ten minutes, will go through to the next round," the umpire declared. "Any goblin hit by a ball will automatically be disqualified."

The girls quickly ducked behind a tree next to the club gates and peeped out.

They saw the umpire
goblin put the Magic
Racquet down carefully
on his chair and go
over to the ball
machine. The other

goblins were all gathered on
the other side of the net.

"One, two, three, go!" the umpire
yelled, switching on the machine.

It immediately began firing tennis
balls at the waiting goblins. Some of
them weren't ready and didn't even
have the chance to lift their racquets
before they were hit by flying balls.

"That's not fair!" one of them
grumbled.

"You're out!" the umpire said sternly.
The goblins who had been hit

trooped sulkily off and began filling up
the seats surrounding the court.
Meanwhile, the
remaining goblins
were batting
and lobbing
the balls away,
and just about
managing
to dodge the
ones they
couldn't return.
   "Look,
Kirsty!" Rachel
nudged her friend.
"What's the umpire
doing?"
   The goblin umpire was
grinning to himself.

As the girls watched, he sneakily flipped a switch on the ball machine and suddenly the balls came flying out of the machine twice as fast. "He's turned the speed of the machine up," Kirsty said with a grin. "You were right, Rachel, he doesn't want any other goblin to get the Magic Racquet, so he's trying to get them all out."

The goblins on the other side of the
net were now whizzing around the
court, whacking the super-fast balls
here and there.

But they hardly had time to hit
one before another was zooming
towards them.

"Hey!" one of the goblins shouted
crossly as he side-stepped a ball.

"What's going on?"

The umpire sniggered. "I said you had to practise your fancy footwork!" he shouted back. And he turned the speed up even higher.

Suddenly, one of the tennis balls spun away from the court and came heading right towards the girls.

"Kirsty, look out!" Rachel cried.

But then a very strange thing happened. The ball stopped suddenly in mid-air and hovered just in front of the tree. A tiny fairy was sitting on top of it, smiling.

"It's Alice the Tennis Fairy!" Kirsty exclaimed.

Tickets, Please!

Alice pushed back her pink visor and waved at Rachel and Kirsty. She wore matching tennis whites and pink and white trainers.

"Girls, I'm glad to see you," Alice said. "I *really* need your help to get my Magic Racquet back."

"We know where your racquet is,"

29

Kirsty replied. "It's on the umpire's chair."
Alice spun round and looked thrilled
as she spotted her pink,
sparkly racquet.
"How can we get
it without being
seen?" she
asked eagerly.
"Any ideas?"
"Maybe we should
sneak into the club while everyone's
distracted by the game," Rachel
suggested.

They all glanced at the court where
the remaining few goblins were still
dashing here and there.

"Good idea," Alice said.

The girls hurried through the
gates, Alice flying alongside them.

"I wonder where all the club members are," Rachel said, as they went down the path towards the clubhouse. "It's amazing that nobody has spotted the goblins yet!"

Alice grinned and pointed her wand at a poster on the clubhouse door. "That's why," she said. "There's a tournament today at Greendale Tennis Club."

"All the members must have gone to take part," Rachel agreed.

As the girls and Alice turned towards the courts, a goblin rushed out of the clubhouse. Immediately Alice hid in Kirsty's pocket.

"Stop!" the goblin shouted. He was wearing a very smart blue uniform with a peaked cap. Dismayed, Rachel and Kirsty came to a halt as the goblin stared suspiciously at them.

"Where are you going?" he snapped.

"We've come to watch the Goblindon tournament," Rachel replied bravely.

The goblin frowned, still looking suspicious. "We don't get many girls coming to watch," he said. "It's mostly just goblins. Where are your tickets?"

Rachel and Kirsty glanced anxiously

at each other. They didn't have
any tickets! But just then Kirsty felt
a tingling sensation in her pocket.
She put her hand inside and,
to her surprise, drew out
two large green tickets.
Alice was peeping out
of the pocket, too,
smiling up at her.

"Here they are,"
Kirsty said cheerfully,
handing them to the goblin.

The goblin peered at the tickets while
Rachel and Kirsty tried to hide their
grins. Both girls had realised that
Alice's fairy magic had produced
the Goblindon tickets just in time.

"These do look official," the goblin
admitted, handing the tickets back.

"OK, you can go in."

Rachel and Kirsty hurried off, breathing sighs of relief.

"Thanks, Alice," Kirsty said as the tiny fairy fluttered out of her pocket. "Your magic tickets worked perfectly."

Meanwhile, Rachel had come to a stop at one of the clubhouse windows.

"Look!" she said, beckoning to Kirsty and Alice. They all peeped through the large window. They could see a huge kitchen where two goblins, wearing aprons and chefs' hats, were serving up strawberries and cream into lots of different bowls.

As the friends watched, the goblins loaded the bowls onto a trolley and rolled it out of the clubhouse.

"Let's follow them and try to get the Magic Racquet back while the goblins are stuffing themselves with strawberries and cream," Kirsty whispered.

Rachel and Alice nodded, and the friends crept towards the tennis courts behind the goblins and the trolley.

Luckily the goblin audience was too caught up in what was happening on the court in front of them to notice the girls. There were only five goblins left now, battling the balls flying from the machine.

"Look, my racquet is still on the umpire's chair," Alice whispered. "I'm going to fly over and try to get it back."

"OK, but be quick, Alice," Kirsty said anxiously. "The ten minutes will be up soon."

Quickly, Alice flew off around the side of the court, keeping out of sight behind the seated goblins.

The umpire blew his whistle. "The first round of Goblindon is now over!" he announced loudly.

The goblins broke into applause and immediately the umpire headed over to his chair.

Rachel and Kirsty stared at each other in horror. Alice was heading towards the chair too, and the goblin umpire might spot her at any moment.

"We have to do something to distract him, Kirsty!" Rachel whispered. "But what?"

Double Distraction

Thinking quickly, Kirsty pulled her Goblindon ticket out of her skirt pocket. "Rachel, have you got a pen?" she asked urgently.

Rachel felt in her pockets. "Will a pencil do?" she said, handing one to her friend.

Kirsty nodded, took the pencil and

rushed across the court to the umpire
goblin, who was nearing his chair.

"May I have your autograph, please?" she asked, holding out the pencil and her ticket. "I think you're the best umpire ever!"

"Oh, me too!" Rachel agreed,
realising what Kirsty was up to,
and pulling out her own ticket.
"Can I have your autograph as well?"

The goblin umpire looked very
proud of himself. "Why, of course!"
he replied with a wide smile.

As the goblin signed Kirsty's ticket, Rachel saw Alice veer away from the umpire's chair and duck behind a shrub, out of sight. Rachel sighed with relief. Kirsty's quick thinking had saved the day, but they still hadn't managed to get hold of the Magic Racquet.

Meanwhile, the umpire had finished signing autographs and was settling himself back in his chair with Alice's racquet on his lap. The girls moved to the side of the court and stood beside the trolley of strawberries and cream. As they did so, they saw one of the five winning goblins removing his white headband, replacing it with a bright orange one.

"Hey, you!" the goblin umpire shouted immediately. "You're only allowed to wear white at Goblindon. You're disqualified!"

"But that's not fair!" the goblin protested.

"Please leave the court," the umpire insisted. "You are disqualified!"

Sulkily the goblin tore off his orange headband and stomped away.

"Right, you four remaining goblins will now play a doubles match," the umpire announced. "Then the winning pair will play each other in the final, and the winner of that game will be Goblindon Champion!"

"Good work, girls," Alice whispered, zooming out of the shrub and slipping inside Kirsty's pocket as the doubles match began. "Maybe we'll get a chance to grab my racquet during this game."

The goblins were speedy and skilful, sending the ball flying across the court at different angles.

"The goblins are playing really well," Rachel murmured.

"It's only because my Magic Racquet is close by," Alice told her, as the smallest goblin dashed forward to return a low volley.

"Uh!" he grunted as he smashed the ball back across the court. Then, as it was played back to him, he hit it again with another loud grunt.

One of the goblins on the other side of  the net turned to the umpire. "He's putting me off by grunting!" the goblin declared furiously.

The umpire pointed at the smallest goblin.

"No grunting allowed at Goblindon,"
he said sternly. "You're disqualified!"

"That's not fair!" the smallest goblin
yelled, storming off the court as the
audience laughed.

His doubles
partner also
looked annoyed.
"I'm on my own
now," he complained.
"Two against one isn't fair."

"Very true," the umpire agreed.
He glanced at the other doubles pair.
"OK, one of you has to be disqualified
too, to even things up."

"Not me," declared one of the
goblins, who had a very large green
nose. "I'm a much better player than
he is." He pointed at his partner.

"That's a fib!" his partner said indignantly. "You're not half as good as I am – your big nose keeps getting in the way of your shots."

"Ooh, you take that back!" the first goblin shouted angrily, running up to the second goblin, who turned and ran away across the court. The first goblin chased after him, trying to bonk him on the head with his racquet.

"This is the strangest tennis tournament I've ever seen!" Rachel laughed as she, Kirsty and Alice watched in amazement.

"Stop!" shouted the umpire. He pointed at the goblin with the big nose. "You're disqualified for using your racquet as a weapon," he snapped. "Leave the court!"

"No!" the goblin said sulkily.

"You can't make me!"

The umpire jumped off the chair, leaving the Magic Racquet on the seat. Rachel, Kirsty and Alice glanced hopefully at each other.

"We might get a chance to grab the racquet if the umpire has to run the other goblin off the court," Kirsty whispered.

"Off! Off! Off!" chanted the crowd.

Muttering, the goblin player gave in and trudged away. To the girls' disappointment, the umpire picked up the racquet again and sat down.

"It's time for the Goblindon Final,"
the umpire announced, and the crowd
broke into applause.

"We're not going to be able to grab
the racquet while the umpire's holding
it," Rachel whispered.

"We'll have
to wait until
the tournament's
over," Kirsty
sighed.

"Yes, maybe we'll
get a chance when they're
celebrating at the end," Alice suggested.

The girls and Alice watched as the
Goblindon Final began. Both goblins
were obviously determined to win, and
they raced around the court, straining
and stretching to return each shot.

The ball went whizzing back and forth so fast, it was a blur.

"This is going to be a very close match," Alice said anxiously. "I just hope it doesn't last too long!"

The fourth game began with a spectacular serve from one of the goblins which the other only just managed to return. The serving goblin then stumbled slightly as he hit his shot. Grinning, the second goblin leapt forward to hit the ball across the court and out of his opponent's reach, but he mistimed his shot and the ball flew into the net.

Instantly, he let out a shriek of rage. "I didn't mean to do that!" he yelled, throwing his racquet to the ground. "Someone moved the net!"

"You're disqualified for improper racquet use," the umpire declared sternly. "A racquet must only be used for hitting things."

"I *did* hit something," the goblin retorted, dancing up and down in fury. "I hit the ground!"

"That doesn't count." The umpire glared at him. "Off!"

As the goblin slunk away, his
opponent punched the air gleefully.
"I won!" he shouted. "I get to be
Keeper of the Magic Racquet!"

The umpire looked down at Alice's
racquet and frowned.

"Look, the umpire doesn't want to
give the racquet away," Rachel
whispered to Alice and Kirsty.

"Actually, you *haven't* won," the
umpire said. "You haven't played
a full match, so there *is* no winner!"

The goblin goggled at
him in disbelief.
"I *can't* play a full
match because
you've disqualified
everyone else!" he
pointed out furiously.

The umpire shrugged. "Well, in that case, *I'm* going to have to remain Keeper of the Magic Racquet myself," he said smugly.

As Rachel watched the goblins arguing, an idea suddenly popped into her head. She turned to Kirsty and Alice. "Whatever I say, disagree with me!" she whispered. Then she rushed over to the umpire's chair.

Kirsty and Alice glanced at each other in excitement and confusion. Rachel obviously had a plan, but what could it be?

A Winning Return

"I think this goblin is right!" Rachel said loudly. "He's the only one left in the tournament, so he should be Keeper of the Magic Racquet!"

The winning goblin looked a bit surprised, but then he grinned. "She's right!" he agreed. "I won fair and square. Hand over the racquet!"

Kirsty smiled to herself as she guessed that Rachel was trying to distract the goblins by getting them to argue with each other. "Don't let the goblins see you, Alice!" she whispered, hurrying over to the umpire.

"Well, I don't agree!" Kirsty said loudly, winking at Rachel. "It's very unfair that the other finalist got disqualified. I mean, he only threw his racquet on the ground. He's the real winner of Goblindon!"

"That's right!" the other finalist cried, darting back onto the court. "I'm a much better player than him. The racquet should be mine!"

"No, it's mine!" his opponent yelled.

"Actually, I thought it was quite unfair that the grunting goblin got disqualified too," Rachel remarked. "Everyone grunts a bit when they're playing sport."

"That's true," shouted the grunting goblin triumphantly as he rushed up to the umpire. "I'm a magnificent player! That Magic Racquet belongs to me!"

By now all the goblins in the seats were streaming onto the court, yelling and complaining. Rachel and Kirsty grinned at each other.

"I was disqualified just because I had an orange headband!" grumbled one goblin.

"Quite right, too!" retorted another.

"Silence!" screamed the umpire. "I'm in charge. My decisions are final!"

"Your decisions are rubbish!" the winning goblin jeered. "You're nothing but a muddle-headed, jelly-brained idiot!"

The umpire looked furious. He leapt down from his chair, leaving the racquet behind, and dashed over to the trolley at

the side of the court. Then he grabbed
a bowl of strawberries and cream and
tipped it over the other goblin's head.

"Help!" the
goblin shrieked
as cream ran
down his face
and the umpire
roared with
laughter.

"Alice, Rachel's
plan has worked!" Kirsty whispered as
the goblins continued to argue amongst
themselves. "Nobody's watching the
Magic Racquet. Can you grab it now?"

Alice nodded and soared up towards
the umpire's chair. None of the goblins
noticed the tiny fairy as she fluttered
down and touched the Magic Racquet.

Rachel and Kirsty watched as the racquet immediately shrank to its Fairyland size, pulsing a deeper pink colour as it did so. Alice snatched the racquet up and did a perfect backhand swing, smiling down at the girls in delight.

Kirsty grinned back. But then one of the goblins gave an angry shout.

"Look, a pesky fairy has got the Magic Racquet!" he yelled. "And I bet those naughty girls helped her to get it, too!"

Game, Set and Match

All the goblins spun round to glare at
Rachel and Kirsty.

Feeling very nervous, the girls backed
away as the goblins advanced.

"Oh, help!" Rachel murmured
anxiously as she came to a halt against
the fence at one end of the court, next
to the ball machine. "Kirsty, I think we

might be trapped!"

Kirsty gulped as she stared at the crowd of angry goblins heading towards them. Frantically, she glanced across the court, looking for inspiration, and her gaze fell on the food trolley.

"Alice!" Kirsty called to the tiny fairy who was hovering above the umpire's chair, looking worried. "Can you whizz the trolley over to us?"

Puzzled, Alice nodded and waved her
wand. Immediately the trolley sped over
to Rachel and Kirsty.

Straightaway, Kirsty began grabbing
bowls of strawberries and cream from
the trolley and tipping them into the
ball machine. Rachel saw what her
friend was doing and rushed to help.
Meanwhile the goblins were still
advancing menacingly.

"Here goes!" Kirsty cried when
all the bowls were empty, and
she turned the machine on.

A second later
a gooey, pink mass
of strawberries
and cream came
shooting out of
the machine.
The goblins
yelped with
surprise as they
were splattered
with the mixture
from head to toe.

"I order you to stop!"
yelled the umpire goblin.
But his words were cut short
as a large blob of strawberries

and cream flew straight into
his mouth. "Urgh!"
The umpire looked
furious, and then he
suddenly beamed
with delight.
"Yum!" he said
happily. "That
tastes lovely!"
And he began
slurping up the
strawberries and
cream from his
hands and arms. 
Rachel and Kirsty
grinned at each other
as the other goblins also
began to realise that the
pink mixture tasted good.

Eagerly they scooped the strawberries and cream off themselves and crammed it greedily into their mouths.

Soon the machine was empty, but the goblins were full.

"Ooh, I'm really stuffed now," groaned the grunting goblin. "My tummy aches!"

"Mine too," the other goblins mumbled, holding their stomachs.

"Time you all went home," said
Alice, smiling kindly at them. "You'll
soon feel better."

The goblins nodded and staggered off,
clutching their bulging tummies.

"Well done, girls!" Alice laughed,
twirling around happily in the air.

"I really thought we were done for until Kirsty had her brilliant idea to put the strawberries and cream in the ball machine!"

"What a mess it made, though," Kirsty laughed, looking down at the squashed strawberries at their feet. "I'll soon fix that," said Alice. And she sent a swirl of fairy magic fizzing across the court, cleaning up the mess in an instant. "My magic has put everything back to normal in the tennis club as well," Alice went on, her eyes twinkling, "so when the members come back they'll never guess that there was a Goblindon tournament here!"

"Thanks, Alice," Rachel said.

"Now I must shoot off to Fairyland and tell everyone the good news." Clutching her racquet, Alice waved to the girls. "Thank you for your help, girls, but don't forget, the Fairyland Olympics start soon and one of the Magic Sporty Objects is still missing."

"We'll do our best to find it," Kirsty promised as Alice blew them a kiss and vanished in a burst of pink sparkles.

"That was a close thing," Kirsty remarked, smiling at Rachel. "We really were outnumbered by goblins today, but we got Alice's racquet back in the end."

"And there's only Gemma the Gymnastics Fairy's Magic Hoop left to find now," Rachel added. "Kirsty, we must find it before the Fairyland Olympics start!"

"Definitely," Kirsty agreed. "But maybe we'd better go home for lunch now. All those strawberries have made me hungry!"

**Now Rachel and Kirsty
must help...**

Gemma the Gymnastics Fairy

Read on for a sneak peek...

"Almost there," Rachel Walker said
as she and her best friend, Kirsty Tate,
walked along the sunny street. "Aunty
Joan lives around the corner, near
my school."

"That's good," Kirsty said, glancing
down at the basket they were carrying.
"These Easter eggs might melt if it was
any further!"

Kirsty was staying with Rachel's
family for a week of the Easter holidays
and the two girls were delivering Easter
gifts to Rachel's cousins.

"I can't believe it's Friday already," Rachel said. "The Fairyland Olympic Games start today!"

Kirsty nodded. "And we still haven't found Gemma the Gymnastics Fairy's Magic Hoop," she said. "If we don't get it back from the goblins soon, then all the gymnastics events at the Olympics will be spoiled."

The girls were having a very exciting week, helping the Sporty Fairies find their missing Magic Sporty Objects. The Magic Sporty Objects ensured that sport was fun and safe for everyone in the human world, as well as in Fairyland, as long as they were with their rightful owners, the Sporty Fairies.

Naughty Jack Frost knew the Magic Sporty Objects were so powerful that they made anyone who was holding them, or even just close to them, very skilled at that particular sport. He had sent his goblins to steal the Sporty Objects so that they could use them to cheat in the Olympic Games and become the winning team. Jack Frost knew that the winners would receive a golden cup full of luck as the big prize – and he really wanted it for himself...

Read Gemma the Gymnastics Fairy
to find out what magic happens next...

Meet the
Friendship Fairies

When Jack Frost steals the Friendship Fairies' magical objects, BFFs everywhere are in trouble! Can Rachel and Kirsty help save the magic of friendship?

www.rainbowmagicbooks.co.uk

RAINBOW magic

Calling all parents, carers and teachers!
The Rainbow Magic fairies are here to help
your child enter the magical world of reading.
Whatever reading stage they are at, there's
a Rainbow Magic book for everyone!
Here is Lydia the Reading Fairy's guide to
supporting your child's journey at all levels.

Starting Out

Our Rainbow Magic Beginner Readers are perfect for first-time readers who are just beginning to develop reading skills and confidence. Approved by teachers, they contain a full range of educational levelling, as well as lively full-colour illustrations.

1

Developing Readers

Rainbow Magic Early Readers contain longer stories and wider vocabulary for building stamina and growing confidence. These are adaptations of our most popular Rainbow Magic stories, specially developed for younger readers in conjunction with an Early Years reading consultant, with full-colour illustrations.

2

Going Solo

The Rainbow Magic chapter books - a mixture of series and one-off specials - contain accessible writing to encourage your child to venture into reading independently. These highly collectible and much-loved magical stories inspire a love of reading to last a lifetime.

3

www.rainbowmagicbooks.co.uk

"Rainbow Magic got my daughter reading chapter books. Great sparkly covers, cute fairies and traditional stories full of magic that she found impossible to put down" – Mother of Edie (6 years)

"Florence LOVES the Rainbow Magic books. She really enjoys reading now" – Mother of Florence (6 years)

The Rainbow Magic Reading Challenge

Well done, fairy friend – you have completed the book!
This book was worth 5 points.

See how far you have climbed on the **Reading Rainbow**
on the Rainbow Magic website below.

The more books you read, the more points you will get,
and the closer you will be to becoming a Fairy Princess!

How to get your Reading Rainbow
1. Cut out the coin below
2. Go to the Rainbow Magic website
3. Download and print out your poster
4. Add your coin and climb up the Reading Rainbow!

There's all this and lots more at
www.rainbowmagicbooks.co.uk

You'll find activities, competitions, stories, a special
newsletter and complete profiles of all the
Rainbow Magic fairies. Find a fairy with your name!

The Sporty Fairies

For Gemma Poole,
with lots of love

Special thanks to
Sue Mongredien

ORCHARD BOOKS

First published in Great Britain in 2008 by Orchard Books
This edition published in 2017 by The Watts Publishing Group

3 5 7 9 10 8 6 4 2

Copyright © 2008 Rainbow Magic Limited.
Copyright © 2008 HIT Entertainment Limited.
Illustrations copyright © Orchard Books, 2008

HiT entertainment

A CIP catalogue record for this book is available from the British Library.

ISBN 978 1 40835 327 1

Printed and bound in Great Britain by Clays Ltd, Elcograf S.p.A.

MIX
Paper from
responsible sources
FSC® C104740

The paper and board used in this book are made from wood from responsible sources

Orchard Books
An imprint of Hachette Children's Group
Part of The Watts Publishing Group Limited
Carmelite House, 50 Victoria Embankment, London EC4Y 0DZ

An Hachette UK Company
www.hachette.co.uk
www.hachettechildrens.co.uk

Gemma
the Gymnastics
Fairy

by Daisy Meadows

Join the **Rainbow Magic Reading Challenge!**

Read the story and collect your fairy points to climb the
Reading Rainbow at the back of the book.

This book is worth 5 points.

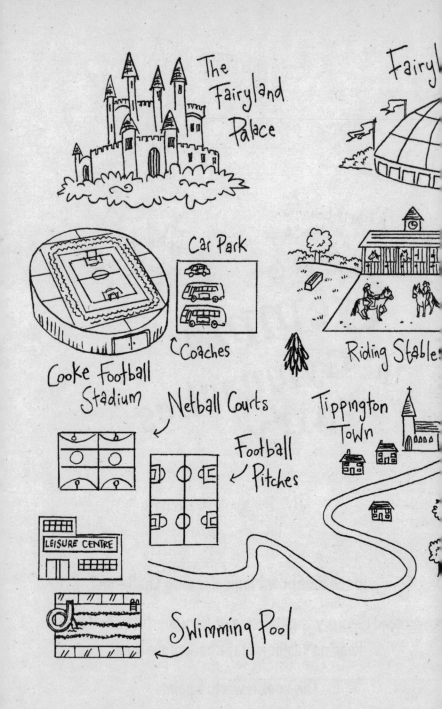

The
Fairyland
Palace

Fairyl

Car Park

Coaches

Cooke Football
Stadium

Netball Courts

Riding Stable

Tippington
Town

Football
Pitches

LEISURE CENTRE

Swimming Pool

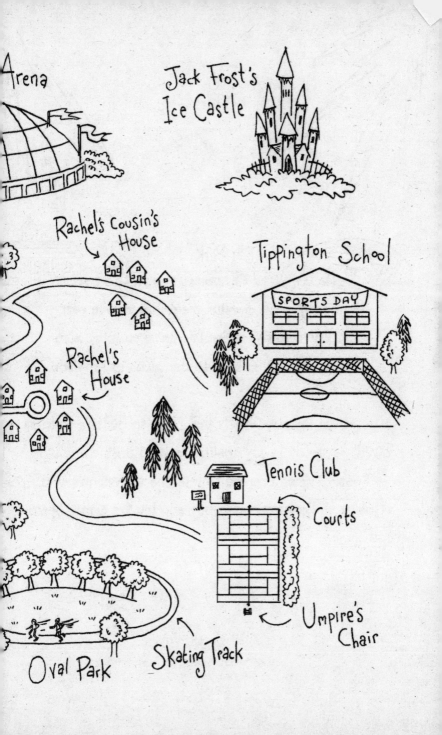

Arena

Jack Frost's Ice Castle

Rachel's Cousin's House

Tippington School

SPORTS DAY

Rachel's House

Tennis Club

Courts

Oval Park

Skating Track

Umpire's Chair

The Fairyland Olympics are about to start,

And my crafty goblins are going to take part.

We'll win this year, for I've got a cunning plan.

I'm sending my goblins to the arena in Fairyland.

The Magic Sporty Objects that make sports safe and fun,

Will be stolen by my goblins, to keep until we've won.

Sporty Fairies, prepare to lose and to watch us win.

Goblins, follow my commands, and let the games begin!

Contents

Someone in School

"Almost there," Rachel Walker said as she and her best friend, Kirsty Tate, walked along the sunny street. "Aunty Joan lives around the corner, near my school."

"That's good," Kirsty said, glancing down at the basket they were carrying. "These Easter eggs might melt if it was any further!"

Kirsty was staying with Rachel's family for a week of the Easter holidays and the two girls were delivering Easter gifts to Rachel's cousins.

"I can't believe it's Friday already," Rachel said. "The Fairyland Olympic Games start today!"

Kirsty nodded. "And we still haven't found Gemma the Gymnastics Fairy's Magic Hoop," she said. "If we don't get it back from the goblins soon, then all

the gymnastics events at the Olympics
will be spoiled."

The girls were having a very exciting
week, helping the Sporty Fairies find
their missing Magic Sporty Objects. The
Magic Sporty Objects ensured that sport
was fun and safe for everyone in the
human world, as well as in Fairyland,
but only if they were with their rightful
owners, the Sporty Fairies.

Naughty Jack Frost knew the Magic
Sporty Objects were so powerful that
they made anyone who was holding
them, or even just close to them, very
skilled at that particular sport. He had
sent his goblins to steal the Sporty
Objects so that they could use them
to cheat in the Olympic Games and
become the winning team. Jack Frost

knew that the winners would receive a golden cup full of luck as the big prize – and he really wanted it for himself.

The goblins had brought the Magic Sporty Objects into the human world to use while they practised their sports. As the Magic Sporty Objects weren't where they were supposed to be, sports in Fairyland and the human world had been disrupted and spoiled.

The girls passed Tippington School, and Kirsty suddenly stopped. "That's strange," she said, staring across the playground. "I've just seen some children inside the school, dressed in green."

"School's closed for the holidays," Rachel told her. "And our uniform is blue and grey."

The same thought struck both girls at
the same time, and
they let out a
gasp. "Goblins!"
cried Rachel.

"If they are
goblins, they
might have
Gemma's Magic

Hoop with them," Kirsty said excitedly.

They gazed at the school, but there
was no sign of anyone in there now.
"Let's drop these Easter eggs off quickly,
then look around properly," Rachel
suggested.

She and Kirsty rushed to Rachel's
aunt's house. They knocked on the door,
but there was no reply, so they set the
basket down in the porch, out of the sun.

Then they hurried back to the school.
The main entrance was locked. "Let's
try round the back," Rachel said,
leading the way. Then she and Kirsty
froze as they heard the sound of
someone whistling.

They peered around the wall to see
a man with his back to them, painting
some bookcases. "It's the caretaker,"
Rachel whispered. "Look, he's left the
door open. Let's sneak in."

Hearts pounding, the girls crept in
through the open door.

"It's very quiet," Kirsty commented.
"Maybe I imagined it."

"Well, let's check out the gym while
we're here," Rachel said.
"Follow me."

Rachel led Kirsty
down a long
corridor until they
reached a door.
"This is where the
gym equipment is
stored," she said.
"We can go
through here into
the gym itself."

She opened the door
and a netball rolled out.

Frowning, Rachel picked it up and went inside. "What a mess!" she said in surprise. "It's never usually like this."

Kirsty followed. A pile of gym mats had been knocked over, there were balls scattered everywhere and some goal posts lay on the floor. Her heart thumped with excitement. People inside the school, mess in the gym cupboard… Something strange was definitely going on!

The girls crossed to the other door,
opened it a crack and peeped out.
Kirsty stifled a gasp. She couldn't
believe her eyes. The gymnasium
was a blur of green. There were
goblins everywhere!

Training Time

The two girls stared in silence.
There were goblins swinging from
the parallel bars, and from rings
that dangled from the ceiling.
Other goblins were leaping over
the vault, dancing along the
balance beam and tumbling
across the floor mats.

"Wow," Kirsty said, unable to drag her eyes away. "They're brilliant! The Magic Hoop must be nearby for all the goblins to be performing so well!"

Rachel nodded. Then her eye was caught by a flash of blue, and she nudged Kirsty. "Look!" she hissed, pointing.

Kirsty turned, and saw a goblin
effortlessly twirling a bright blue hoop
around one arm. The hoop shimmered
with blue sparkles. "That definitely looks
like fairy magic," she breathed excitedly.

The goblin set the
hoop rolling across
one of the gym
mats, while he
performed a
series of flawless
back flips
alongside it.
Then he landed on
his feet, grabbed the hoop and bowed
deeply to an imaginary audience.

"That must be Gemma's hoop,"
Rachel whispered. "The last Magic
Sporty Object!"

"There's something sparkling in here, too," Kirsty said, suddenly noticing a tiny flash of light in a dark corner.

Rachel turned to see Gemma the Gymnastics Fairy come spiralling up out of a pile of hoops, in a burst of yellow sparkles.

Gemma wore a pale blue leotard and yellow tights. Her hair was coiled up in a bun, and her wings were tipped with gold.

"Hello, Gemma!" Kirsty said in delight. "Perfect timing – we think we've spotted your hoop."

Gemma beamed. "Hurrah!" she said. "I've just come from Fairyland, where all the athletes are busy with their last-minute practice sessions. The opening celebrations for the Olympics will be starting soon. We just have to get my hoop back in time!"

"Yes, the goblins are practising too," Kirsty remarked.

But Rachel was lost in thought. Gemma's and Kirsty's words had given her an idea. "That's it!" she cried. "We could help the goblins practise!"

Kirsty stared at her, wondering if she'd heard correctly. "Help the goblins?" she repeated in surprise.

Rachel grinned. "If we offer to train the goblins, we'll have a good chance of getting close to Gemma's hoop," she explained.

Gemma cartwheeled through the air.

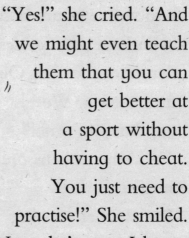

"Yes!" she cried. "And we might even teach them that you can get better at a sport without having to cheat. You just need to practise!" She smiled. "Now, let's see…I know how I can help." She waved her wand at the girls, and golden fairy dust streamed around them. Then, in the twinkling of an eye, their clothes changed.

24

Rachel and Kirsty looked at each other
and smiled. They were now wearing
matching tracksuits and trainers, with
stopwatches on their wrists. Their hair
had been swept up into ponytails, and
there were silver whistles around their
necks. Peaked caps
helped to hide the
girls' faces, so that
the goblins
wouldn't easily
see through their
disguise. "Look
at our T-shirts!"
Kirsty giggled,
pointing. Rachel looked
down and saw that "K & R Goblin
Training Team" was written in glittery
silver letters across her chest.

Gemma flew up to perch on Kirsty's ponytail, where her wings made her look rather like a shiny hair bow. "Now to start training those goblins," she said. "And get the Magic Hoop!"

"Let's go," Kirsty agreed. And she and Rachel pushed open the doors and strode into the gym, blowing their whistles loudly.

The goblins all stopped in surprise. One goblin was so startled, he lost concentration during his floor routine and tumbled head over heels onto the crash mat. He picked himself up and shuffled over to another goblin. "Who are they?" the girls heard him whisper.

"All right, goblins!" shouted Kirsty. "This is your last chance to get in shape before the Fairyland Olympics! And we're going to help you, so line up in front of me! Move it! Move it!"

Rachel held her breath. For their plan to work, the goblins had to want her and Kirsty to help with their training. But none of the goblins had moved a muscle to line up. Was the plan doomed before it had even started?

Gymnastic Fantastic

"Come on!" Rachel cried, clapping her hands. "You don't want those fairies to beat you in the Olympics, do you? We're here to make you gymnastic fantastic, so that you have a chance of winning gold medals!"

"I want a medal!" one goblin called out from the crowd, running to start a line in front of Kirsty.

"Me too!" cried another.

"And me, and me!" called some
of the other goblins, as they jostled
to get in line.

The one with the Magic Hoop was
in the middle and demanded that the
others give him more room. "Look at
me!" he cried, swivelling the hoop
around his hips at lightning speed.

"We want you all to practise your back flips first," Rachel said. "You can demonstrate," she added, pointing at the goblin with the Magic Hoop.

She held her breath as the goblin walked to the edge of the mat. She'd noticed the way he'd let go of the hoop when he'd practised his back flips earlier. If he did the same thing again, she might be able to grab it!

As Rachel had hoped, the goblin set the Magic Hoop rolling before flipping along next to it.  Unfortunately, the hoop whizzed along so fast, it was impossible for Rachel and Kirsty to even think about running to catch it. And as soon as the goblin had finished, he snatched it up again.

Kirsty and Rachel exchanged glances. They'd have to try again later.

"OK, who's next?" Rachel asked.

"Me! Me! ME!" shouted the goblins, trying to push each other out of the way.

Kirsty blew her whistle. "It's you
next," she decided, pointing to a goblin
with a pointy chin. "Off you go!"

One by one, the goblins took turns
to perform their back flips across the
floor. They weren't quite as good as
the goblin with the Magic Hoop, but
they all tried hard.

Meanwhile, the goblin with the
Magic Hoop was showing off to
a group of goblins in a corner of
the gym. "Watch this!" he yelled,
breaking into a run across the gym
floor. He ran to the gym horse and
vaulted over it, tossing the hoop high
into the air as he did so. He turned
a perfect somersault and then landed

feet-first through the falling hoop.

Everyone burst into applause,
including Kirsty, Rachel and Gemma.

"He won't be able to do that in the
Olympic contest," Rachel heard one
goblin mutter to another. "Jack Frost
is going to shrink the hoop really
small so the judges don't know he's
got it. Clever, huh?"

Gemma bristled
with annoyance.
"I can't bear
cheating," she
whispered to
Kirsty. "It makes
me feel sick!"

But watching the
performance had given
Kirsty an idea. "Let's make an obstacle
course for the goblins," she suggested.
"You saw how the goblin had to throw
the Magic Hoop when he vaulted.
Well, there are other gym moves where
he'd have to let it go, too."

Rachel's eyes lit up. "Yes," she said,
"and we could even end the course
with a ring toss – where the goblins
have to throw a hoop over me or you.

Then the goblin with the Magic Hoop will have to throw it right to us!"

"Brilliant!" cried Gemma, in her silvery voice. "Let's put the plan into action!"

Overcoming Obstacles

Kirsty blew her whistle again. "You did a great job on your back flips," she told the goblins. "Now we're going to set up an obstacle course for you. Please practise your forward and backward rolls while we do that."

The goblins immediately began rolling around on the floor, pausing every so often to argue with each other.

Meanwhile, Kirsty and Rachel quickly arranged some pieces of equipment to make an obstacle course, then Rachel clapped her hands to get the goblins' attention. "This is what you need to do," she said. "Start by walking on your hands along the balance beam. Then run over to the parallel bars and do three somersaults."

"Next," Kirsty said, "you turn upside down on the rings, vault over the horse and tumble across the mat while twirling a ribbon."

"Finally," Rachel explained, "each of you has to toss a hoop over Kirsty,

who'll be standing at the other
end of the gym." She held up her
stopwatch. "I'll time you all.
I wonder who'll be the fastest?"

"I'll be the fastest," a tall goblin
boasted. "You wait!"

"No way!" a goblin with big ears
argued. "I'll be faster than you."

Kirsty pointed to a small goblin at
the front. "You can go first," she said
encouragingly. "Ready,
steady, go!"

Rachel started her
stopwatch as the
small goblin set off.
He flipped into a
handstand and
carefully walked
along the balance beam.

His legs wobbled slightly but he
managed not to fall. Then he ran to
the parallel bars and performed three
somersaults — but he was
enjoying himself so
much that he
kept on going.
"Wheeee!" he
squealed, whizzing round.
"OK, onto the rings now," Rachel
reminded him.

The goblin swung upside-down on
the rings, then vaulted over the horse.
Then he grabbed a ribbon and began
a series of cartwheels and handsprings
across the mat, spiralling the ribbon as
he went. Unfortunately, he lost his
balance several times, and dropped his
ribbon once on the last section.

"Not to worry," Rachel said. "We can work on that later. Now grab a hoop from the pile, stand behind the line and take your best shot."

The goblin took a hoop, steadied himself and then threw it towards Kirsty. The hoop bounced off Kirsty's arm and clattered to the floor.

"Good try," Kirsty called.

"Your time was three minutes, thirty seconds," Rachel told him. "Next!"

It took a while for all the goblins to go through the course. The goblin with the Magic Hoop insisted on going last. "What's the fastest time so far?" he asked as he stood at the starting line.

"Two minutes, forty seconds," Rachel replied.

The goblin looked scornful. "I'll beat that easily!" he declared.

"Ready, steady, go!" Rachel called, blowing her whistle.

Off went the goblin, mounting the beam with a spectacular leap. He tossed the hoop into the air as he went into

a handstand and caught it on one foot, balancing it perfectly as he moved along the beam. "Wow!" Kirsty muttered under her breath to Gemma. "That's impressive."

At the end of the beam, the goblin dismounted with a double back flip, sending the hoop flying into the air. As he landed, he caught it neatly and then ran on to the parallel bars.

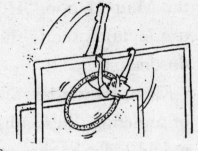

With the hoop looped over one shoulder, he did three perfect somersaults at dizzying speed.

It was quite a show. The goblin whizzed through the rest of the obstacle course without a single mistake. The other goblins watched open-mouthed, too amazed even to argue with each other.

He was making record time when he came to the last part of the challenge – the ring toss. He looked suspiciously at Kirsty and held tight to the Magic Hoop. "Hoop-tossing is not a gymnastic sport," he said. "I shan't do this bit."

Kirsty bit her lip. She had to think of something fast, otherwise their plan would fail! She shrugged. "Oh, dear," she said pityingly. "Are you worried you won't be as good as the others?"

"No way!" the goblin snapped.
"Watch this!" And he tossed the hoop
high into the air.

The girls and Gemma held their
breath as it spun in mid-air above
Kirsty's head...

Frost in Fairyland

The hoop landed perfectly over Kirsty's head and the goblins all burst into a round of applause.

The goblin who'd thrown it smirked and bowed and then walked towards Kirsty as if to take it back.

But Kirsty was too quick for him. She stepped out of the hoop, picked it

up and held it in the air for Gemma,
who zoomed down to it immediately.
As soon as Gemma's fingers closed
around it, the hoop magically shrank
down to its Fairyland size. Then
Gemma touched it with her wand,
and there was a flash of golden
sparkles. The hoop's magic was
working properly again!

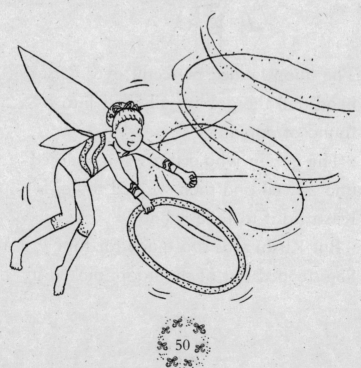

"Hey!" cried one of the goblins.
"It's one of those meddling fairies – and
she's got our hoop!"

"Someone get it back!" yelled another
goblin. "Otherwise we'll never win
anything at the Olympics!"

The goblins all made a mad dash for
the girls and Gemma, clambering over
each other in their
rush to get the
hoop. Kirsty
and Rachel
looked at
one another
in alarm
as the mob
of angry
goblins surged
towards them,

but Gemma waved her wand and
turned the girls into fairies,
just in time. Rachel's
heart thumped as she
fluttered out of the
goblins' reach.
That was close!
   Gemma waved
her wand again,
and all the
pieces of gym
equipment
sparkled with
thousands of tiny
golden lights before
dancing back into
their rightful places in
the store room. The
goblins watched in

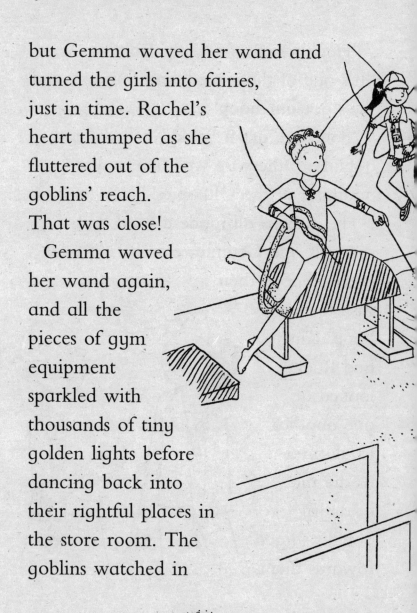

bewilderment, their eyes wide. As the last hoop rolled away, Gemma grinned at them. "See you in Fairyland," she said. "Don't be late – or you'll miss the opening ceremony of the Olympics!" Before any of the goblins could reply, Gemma had waved her wand a third time, and she and the girls were swept up in a magical whirlwind.

"Off we go to Fairyland!" Kirsty
and Rachel heard her call merrily.

A few seconds later, the girls felt
themselves float down to land, and the
whirlwind cleared.

"We're in the Fairyland Arena
again!" Kirsty declared.

Rachel whistled. "And look how
full it is."

The girls had been in the arena
once already, on the first day of this
adventure. But then it had been
completely empty, whereas now the
seats were filled with excited-looking
fairies, elves, pixies and goblins, all
chattering about the Olympics.

Kirsty could quite happily have
spent ages gazing around at the sights.
A tall green frog was selling official
programmes on one row. A group
of pixie cheerleaders danced in the
centre of the arena. And the spectators
all waved colourful flags and banners
to show which contestants they
were supporting. Some of the flags
were magical and kept changing
colour. Some even seemed to be
playing tunes!

They'd landed at the side of the arena and Gemma led them to the centre, where the Fairy King and Queen greeted them warmly. Then the King handed Gemma a sparkly gold microphone, so that she could speak to the crowd.

"Hello, everyone," Gemma said, waving. "I'm pleased to announce that Kirsty and Rachel have now helped us get all the

Magic Sporty Objects back, including my Magic Hoop!"

A huge cheer went up from the spectators, but not from the watching goblins. They looked decidedly fed up at the news. But the fairies, pixies, elves and other magical people were all clapping, cheering and waving their flags with joy.

The King and Queen looked delighted, too. "Thank you," King Oberon said to Kirsty and Rachel. "You have helped save our Olympic Games! Without you, the goblins would have had an unfair advantage."

"Now that the Magic Sporty Objects are back with our Sporty Fairies, the games will be fairly contested," Queen Titania smiled.
"We are very grateful."

Kirsty and Rachel curtsied, feeling very proud. But then the air turned cold. Rachel shivered and rubbed her arms. "Where's that wind coming from?" she asked,

as an icy gale blew through the arena.

"There's frost on the ground!" Kirsty exclaimed, pointing to the white sparkly crystals at their feet.

Everyone stared up at the sky as a figure approached, speeding through the air.

"It's Jack Frost!" Rachel realised in dismay.

Beginnings and Endings

Jack Frost landed in the arena and stamped his feet. "If it hadn't been for you interfering, I'd have won the Olympics this year," he snarled at Kirsty and Rachel. "The golden cup of luck would have been mine!"

The Queen gave him a stern look. "Your team will have to play by the rules like every other team in the games," she told him.

Jack Frost ignored her and advanced on the girls, his wand raised. "I'm fed up with you two messing up my plans," he shouted. He pointed his wand at them. "So now I'm going to—"

"You're not going to do anything!" the Queen interrupted, waving her own wand. The crowd gasped as Jack Frost's wand flew straight into the Queen's hand.

"I'll look after this while the games are taking place," she told Jack Frost firmly. "I'm not going to let you disrupt the Olympics any further!"

Jack Frost scowled at her, but without his wand he could do nothing except turn and storm off to the spectators' area.

"He knows when he's beaten," Gemma said in a low voice.

"And now the games can begin!" the King declared.

Gemma winked at the girls. "That's my cue," she said, and shot up into the air. She was joined by the other six Sporty Fairies – Helena, Francesca, Zoe, Naomi, Samantha and Alice – and they all spiralled up towards the clouds.

Rachel and Kirsty watched as they then flew back to the arena in an amazing rainbow of colour. They sprinkled fairy dust over the athletes lining up for the opening parade, then wrote "GOOD LUCK!" in large glittery letters in the sky.

"Please be upstanding for the singing of the Fairyland Olympic Anthem," Queen Titania said, and the audience rose to their feet.

A goblin walked to the centre of the stage, with a microphone in his hand. He cleared his throat and began to sing.

Rachel elbowed Kirsty and grinned. "It's the goblin we met when we helped Rebecca the Rock 'n' Roll Fairy," she whispered. "Remember?"

Kirsty nodded. "Yes, the one who loved to sing Elvis songs!" she said with a grin.

The goblin made a sweeping bow
as he finished singing, and the crowd
cheered — Rachel and Kirsty loudest
of all.

Then the Queen presented the girls
with a glittering silver wand. "Girls, we
would be honoured if you would light
the Olympic flame for us," she said.
"And there are some fairies who would
love to help you…"

As she finished speaking, Rachel and
Kirsty both gasped. Flying into the
arena was Ruby the Red Fairy,
the first fairy they'd ever met, with her
Rainbow sisters. Behind them came all
the Weather Fairies, and then Katie the
Kitten Fairy flew in, waving at the
girls as she was joined by the other
Pet Keeper Fairies. More and more of

the girls' fairy friends kept flying into the arena.

Kirsty couldn't stop smiling as she greeted them all. "I think every fairy we've ever helped is here with us," she said happily to Rachel.

Rachel had a lump in her throat. "It's so nice to see you again!" she said, throwing her arms around Lucy the Diamond Fairy.

Once all the fairies had arrived, the Queen commanded them to touch their wands together, along with the silver wand that Rachel and Kirsty were holding.

Rachel held her breath as all the wands came together. A spark appeared at the end of the special silver wand.

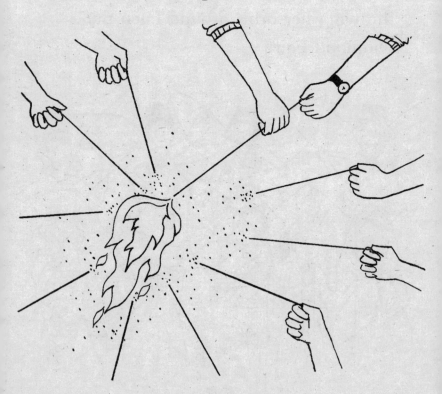

Then the other fairies moved aside
and the girls took the lit wand towards
a sparkling silver cauldron.
They touched the flame
to the cauldron,
and, in a flash of
rainbow-coloured
sparkles, a
roaring flame
flared up and
then settled
down to burn steadily.
There was a round of
applause from the crowd
and the fairies flew up into the air
again, calling out their goodbyes.
King Oberon and Queen Titania
came over to the girls. "It's time for
you to go home now," the King said,

"but you'll find one last surprise waiting for you there."

"Thank you," Kirsty said, curtseying.
"We've really enjoyed helping the Sporty Fairies," added Rachel. "We're all very grateful to you," the Queen said. "Goodbye, girls!" "Goodbye!" Rachel and Kirsty replied.

Then the King waved his wand, and the girls were swept up in a whirlwind and carried gently home.

They found themselves outside Rachel's school, in their normal clothes, each holding a gold sparkly envelope.

Kirsty opened hers eagerly, as did
Rachel. Inside they found glittering
silver tickets. "'*All-access pass to
the Fairyland Olympics*'," Kirsty
read aloud.

"Wow!" Rachel said, beaming.
"We can go to any event we like."

"Oh!" Kirsty marvelled. "What
a great surprise!"

A light gust of wind made the tickets flutter in their fingers, and they heard Gemma's silvery voice carried on the breeze. "All you have to do is hold your ticket and wish, and you'll be back at the Fairyland Arena," she whispered.

Kirsty and Rachel smiled in delight. "I'm so pleased we'll get to see the events," Rachel said happily, as they started to walk home.

"Me too," Kirsty agreed. "I especially want to see how the goblin gymnastics team perform. After all, they did have some excellent coaching!"

Now it's time for Kirsty and Rachel to help...

Poppy the Piano Fairy

Read on for a sneak peek...

"Ooh, I love to dance!" Rachel Walker sang along to the radio, pretending her hairbrush was a microphone. "When I hear the music, my toes start tapping and my fingers start snapping – I just love to dance!"

Kirsty Tate, Rachel's best friend, grinned and grabbed her own hairbrush.

"I can't stop dancing!" she chorused. "Just can't stop dancing!"

The girls tried to do a complicated dance routine as they sang, but then Kirsty went left and Rachel went right and they ended up bumping into each other. Laughing, they collapsed onto Kirsty's bedroom carpet.

"It's really hard to sing and dance at the same time," said Rachel as the song ended.

"I know," Kirsty agreed. "I don't think we'd be very good in a band, Rachel!"

"That was The Sparkle Girls with their new single, *Can't Stop Dancing*," the radio DJ announced as Kirsty and Rachel sat up. "And if anyone out there thinks they could make it big as a pop star too, why not come along and audition for the National Talent Competition next weekend?"

Rachel and Kirsty glanced at each other.

"That sounds cool!" Rachel said.

"One lucky singer or band will win a recording contract with MegaBig Records," the DJ went on. "So remember – come along to the New Harmony Mall next weekend, and maybe one day I'll be playing *your* songs on my show!"

"The New Harmony Mall is only a few miles from Wetherbury," Kirsty said. "I'm sure Mum or Dad would take us to watch the competition if we asked them..."

Read Poppy the Piano Fairy to find out what adventures are in store for Kirsty and Rachel!

Meet the
Friendship Fairies

When Jack Frost steals the Friendship Fairies' magical objects, BFFs everywhere are in trouble! Can Rachel and Kirsty help save the magic of friendship?

www.rainbowmagicbooks.co.uk

RAINBOW magic

Calling all parents, carers and teachers!
The Rainbow Magic fairies are here to help
your child enter the magical world of reading.
Whatever reading stage they are at, there's
a Rainbow Magic book for everyone!
Here is Lydia the Reading Fairy's guide to
supporting your child's journey at all levels.

Starting Out

Our Rainbow Magic Beginner Readers are perfect for first-time readers who are just beginning to develop reading skills and confidence. Approved by teachers, they contain a full range of educational levelling, as well as lively full-colour illustrations.

Developing Readers

Rainbow Magic Early Readers contain longer stories and wider vocabulary for building stamina and growing confidence. These are adaptations of our most popular Rainbow Magic stories, specially developed for younger readers in conjunction with an Early Years reading consultant, with full-colour illustrations.

Going Solo

The Rainbow Magic chapter books – a mixture of series and one-off specials – contain accessible writing to encourage your child to venture into reading independently. These highly collectible and much-loved magical stories inspire a love of reading to last a lifetime.

www.rainbowmagicbooks.co.uk

"Rainbow Magic got my daughter reading chapter books. Great sparkly covers, cute fairies and traditional stories full of magic that she found impossible to put down" - Mother of Edie (6 years)

"Florence LOVES the Rainbow Magic books. She really enjoys reading now" - Mother of Florence (6 years)

The Rainbow Magic Reading Challenge

Well done, fairy friend – you have completed the book!
This book was worth 5 points.

See how far you have climbed on the **Reading Rainbow**
on the Rainbow Magic website below.

The more books you read, the more points you will get,
and the closer you will be to becoming a Fairy Princess!

How to get your Reading Rainbow
1. Cut out the coin below
2. Go to the Rainbow Magic website
3. Download and print out your poster
4. Add your coin and climb up the Reading Rainbow!

There's all this and lots more at
www.rainbowmagicbooks.co.uk

You'll find activities, competitions, stories, a special
newsletter and complete profiles of all the
Rainbow Magic fairies. Find a fairy with your name!